MW01136709

MOUNTAIN MISERY

CALAVERAS LOVE STORIES

Steve
Thanks for
being a friend
and putting up with
Pat all these years!
Happy Trails
Lisa Michelle

For Charlie,
and all who take comfort
in another's misery

Chamaebatia, better known as "mountain misery," is a pungent low-growing shrub that smothers much of the forest floor in Calaveras County. Hard to kill, dense, and of little nutritional value, the dark-green tangle thrives while leaving its mark—a sticky resin that reeks and turns black—on everything it touches.

SAN ANDREAS

Shawn rolled through the bus terminal, past stifling diesel fumes, past whores and hobos, and found his way to Louie's. The place was mostly empty except for the pickled blonde at the end of the bar. Long ash hung like a talon from the Pall Mall pinched between her fingers. Her Aqua Net bouffant keeping rhythm with "American Pie" rattling the blown speakers on the Wurlitzer.

A third whiskey on the rocks seemed to settle Shawn's nerves. He hadn't been this scared since Vietnam. As soon as the flashbacks surfaced, he shoved them into the deepest, darkest part of himself. With a meaty index finger, he scratched at the stitches in his brow, then pushed his Stetson away from long, dark sideburns. The Trailways bus ticket glared at him from across his table. Reno, Nevada, to San Andreas, California. Departing at 4:10. He had thirty minutes to get on that bus.

"Bye, bye, Miss American Pie . . ." sang the Basque bartender in an accent that helped mask the hint of a speech impediment. He would have looked plain if not for the red beret placed like a cherry on his grizzled head. Clouds of lemon Pledge engulfed the mahogany bar as he sprayed and polished in tiny circles. Shawn caught the old Basque occasionally peeking up at him. He quit polishing when Shawn raised his tired blue eyes along with an empty glass.

The Basque flung his waxy rag over his shoulder, then brought a jug from under the bar. Cradling it like a newborn, he hobbled to the table. "You look like him." The Basque offered a sympathetic grin while pointing his thumb at the Marlboro Man on the cigarette machine. With a grunt, Shawn slid his glass closer to the Basque.

"This very good drink. I make." The Basque poured two fingers of the amber into the glass. "I see you here, during rodeo, before . . ." His face furrowed and looked upward, he seemed to be struggling for the right words. Shawn looked down at the mud and manure dried on his boots. Looked down at the heels where spurs had scarred the leather. He felt the paralyzing pain and quickly raised his glass.

"May the road rise up to meet ya." He downed the drink in two gulps.

"No!" The Basque squeezed his beret. "*Kaka zaharra*—too much strong, drink slow."

The afterburn of the home brew hit hard. Shawn smacked and squeezed his thighs with all his strength and felt nothing. He leaned back. "Know the difference between a man who wants to drink and a man who wants to get drunk?"

"Perhaps . . . Maybe . . . No."

"You should." A grin lifted the corner of his mouth.

"Shawn." He offered his hand to the Basque.

"Louie." His grip was firm as he took Shawn's hand with gnarled fingers. "You win rodeo here?" He admired Shawn's silver-and-gold buckle. "Is beautiful."

Shawn tilted his 1971 Reno Rodeo buckle. He studied the upside-down bucking horse and smirked. "Yep. I was the champ this year." He unsnapped the buckle from his belt and set it on the table. "I need to call my wife. Let me use your phone, and it's yours."

Louie smiled and turned. "You keep. I bring phone. Is no problem for good customer."

Louie fumbled with the phone, then untangled the long cord as he dragged it to Shawn's table. "Okay, you call, I see if my lamb is cook." Louie tapped the ticket with his middle finger. "You go home?" he asked, but it sounded more like advice than a question.

"Hope so. Ain't up to me," Shawn said as Louie pushed through a swinging door. Hints of lamb escaped and mingled with the blonde's Pall Malls. The stench caused Shawn's insides to want out. He took two deep breaths, waited for courage that never came, then snatched up the receiver.

His finger settled just outside the numbered holes in the dial. Every discouraging return of the rotary offered a chance to hang up. The muscles in his jaw flexed as he gritted his teeth and dialed the last number. For the first time in a long time, he asked God to lend a hand. Just this once, and he'd never ask for anything ever again.

The ring was long and loud on the line, and Shawn pinched the bridge of his nose. It rang nine times before he started to hang up. He heard her and dropped his head to meet the receiver.

3

"Hello?" There was an urgency in her voice. "Hello?" Sweet and innocent.

"It's me."

A long silence confirmed the distance between them.

"You there? Ruth?"

"Figured you was dead . . . or got a gal. And you ain't dead."

"Not yet."

"Go to hell."

He knew the way she hid hurt behind anger. "It ain't nothin' like that, and you know it."

"I can't do this."

"Hon, I—"

"You think you can just take off and rodeo all summer, leave me and Joey here and not call for nearly three weeks." Her voice cracked. "There's *no* excuse."

"I know."

"Every night, he says, 'Where Daddy, where Daddy?' Know what I tell him?"

"I don't know," Shawn whispered.

"*Exactly!* 'I don't know.' Then we cry ourselves to sleep, Shawn. Thought I was all cried out." Ruth scolded him between sobs, "Ain't fair stickin' it all on me. I can't keep up with the house and the feedin'. The irrigatin' alone takes most the day!" She slurped a jagged breath. "Oh, and I've lost track of how many calves are coughin', two died last week."

"I'm so, so sorry. Goddamn it. I just wanted—" He dropped his head, pulled the brim of his hat down. His eyes stung as tears disappeared into the black tablecloth.

"You wanted what? Tell me, Shawn. *What?*"

"I wanted my boy to have a world champion for a

dad." He realized how dopey it sounded and had to defend it. "Not some broke cowpuncher who never did shit—like my pop."

"What's wrong with you? That is *such* a load of bullshit! You rodeo because you love it. You love the admiration—the cheers. You love being on the road with your friends more than being home with your family. Be honest."

He'd gone years and managed to avoid analyzing the awful truth. "I fucked up." Together, they cried, argued about mistakes that had been made, all the regrets and broken promises, then agreed the love was still there, and they cried some more until little Joey's laughter consoled them. "Oh jeez, can I talk to him?" Shawn smiled.

"Come here, Daddy's on the phone, come talk to Daddy, Joey," Ruth insisted.

"Daa-ddy. Daa-ddy, Daa-ddy," Joey sang.

"Yeah, it's Daddy. Whatcha doin', boy? I miss you. Wanna go tractor?"

"Traa-tor. Traa-tor."

"Yeah, tractor. I love you, Joey. Hear me? I love you more than anything." Shawn heard the phone hit the wood floor.

Ruth laughed into the phone. "You should *not* have said tractor. Now he's at the door tryin' to pull his boots on the wrong feet." He pictured her crooked grin that exposed the odd dimple closer to her chin than her cheek. Pictured himself kissing it. Now, he would give anything to live the rest of his life with her and Joey.

"I wanna come home. For good. No more rodeos—swear to God, hon. I miss you guys so bad."

"Where are you?"

5

"Reno. Could be in San Andreas tomorrow—have Ray drive me home."

"By suppertime?"

"Heck yeah."

"Hmmm. Well, I have a surprise for you. And a huge pot roast that needs cookin'. Sure hate to waste it."

"Good. Because, uh . . . I'd like to bring my buddy, if that's okay?" Swiping hard at his eyes with the back of his hand, Shawn wanted to stop the conversation there—say nothing more than, *I'm coming home*, and leave it at that.

"Of course. Who is it?"

His words stuck. "My buddy . . . He, uh . . ." Shawn cleared his throat. "The guy got hurt real bad in Reno. Trails End flipped over on him. Remember the horse broke Charlie Thompkin's legs?"

"Oh yeah. Thought Leo was gonna cull him."

"Well, he sure shoulda. But he didn't, and the son of a bitch did it again, only this time he severed the guy's spinal cord from the waist down. Just like that, the poor bastard's all done. Gonna be in a wheelchair rest of his life."

"Oh my God, you saw it?"

"Yeah. It was bad."

"That's horrible."

"Worst is, he ain't got nowhere to go, so . . . I told him he could stay with us."

She hesitated too long. Fear crawled out of his belly, slithered up his throat. He grabbed his mouth with his palm and waited.

"Gosh, Shawn." She paused. "I don't know. I was gonna surprise you, but I may as well tell you—I'm pregnant." The long silence was sickening. "I can't

6

keep up now." She started to cry. "I'm sorry, I just don't think it's a good idea." Ruth freed a deep, sorrowful sigh. "Really, though, Shawn, it's not fair to Joey. Or me. I mean . . . why would you put this burden on us? On *me*?" Anger reared its ugly head. "It's kinda selfish when you think about it. I've done everything for you and it's never enough. Never! Now you want me to take care of your cripple friend too? You make these decisions and *don't even* consider me or Joey."

She was right. Until now, he hadn't. His heart splintered against his chest, felt like it just might explode—he wished it would. Dying would be so much easier. He had rehearsed the lines for two days, knew them well, just had to force them out fast. "Sell the place." His voice became deep, theatrical. "Get a hold of Ray and have him sell the cattle and horses."

"What? Why?"

"I love you, Ruthie, more than you'll ever know." He swallowed the lump bloating in his throat. "You deserve better."

"What are you—"

He hung up, forgot to breathe while he wadded up the ticket to San Andreas and crushed it in his hand.

"Ain't love grand?" The blonde never looked at Shawn, just jiggled the ice cubes in her gin and tonic before sucking it down.

Shawn's head fell back. He ran his hands up and down his face. Dragged in the deepest, slowest breath he could. Then, with a trembling grasp, released the brake on his wheelchair and spun it toward the door.

MOUNTAIN RANCH

Ray tore the blankets off Ruth. "Breakfast sure ain't gonna cook itself." It wasn't his slow baritone that interrupted the serenity of a dream, it was the cold that ripped Ruth away from a sunny day and people she loved. Lots of people. Friends. Ray flipped the light on before leaving the bedroom, and Ruth hid her eyes in the pillow. The dreary February morning spurred her arthritis. Made turning seventy-five just another day to get through. She stood on the cold wood floor, toes bent outward, knotty joints, crinkled skin, and warped nails. Nothing like the pretty petite feet she once knew. She was sorry she had wasted those good feet on Ray. Sorry she wasted her good years waiting for things to get better. Things never get better, they just sort of subside. Ruth wrapped herself in her robe and a heavy dose of winter stoicism on the way to the bathroom.

The toilet seat was up as usual, and as Ruth swatted it down, she stepped in a wet spot. Ray's aim was always off. *Rotten SOB.* She refused to clean it up today. A hand towel over the spot did the trick. But she

8

was *not* going to pick up the towel. Not today. Today she wore her clean jeans and a gray wool sweater that was usually saved for special occasions but mostly funerals.

Snow swirled outside the window above the kitchen sink. Ruth moved the curtain, raised herself onto her toes, and squinted. "Looks like, what, six inches, maybe?"

Ray, baked hard by the sun and bad luck, slurped runny eggs through his few remaining teeth. "You fill the wood box?"

"Yes." Ruth poured herself another cup of coffee from the old percolator. Ray Peterson refused innovations. Since buying the color television in 1988, he hadn't purchased more than parts for the tractor or the truck. None of those cellular telephones. No satellite television, or World Wide Web hogwash. All of it was a ridiculous waste of time. Meals were made in or on the stove the way they should be. "Microwaves were invented by the Japs to infect us with cancer for kicking their ass in the Second World War," he'd say.

Ruth disagreed with most everything Ray believed, but it was easier to keep quiet and clean house.

"You get my chew when you were in town yesterday?"

"Ughhh. I forgot," Ruth confessed.

"Goddamn it!" Ray slammed his fist on the table. "You didn't forget."

Ruth filled Ray's coffee mug. "I was in a hurry—had to get to the bank before they closed. They said we were overdrawn again and—"

"Double dumb fuck." Ray mopped his plate with his

toast and shoved it in his mouth.

Ruth tightened her grip on the percolator handle. Imagined pouring hot coffee on Ray's lap, then cracking his skull with the pot. The possibility of heaven and hell stopped her. It always stopped her—particularly when suicide seemed the most practical. She'd think of her son, Joey, and of the possibility of seeing him again after twenty years. She'd stop herself the moment her mind wandered to her daughter, Jessica, or Shawn, the father of her children, or the way things should have been—if he hadn't left. Lacking real friends, money, or job skills, leaving was unimaginable. Ruth set the percolator on the table and sat to eat.

"You can just trot your fat ass back to town today."

"It's my birthday, you know. I was thinkin', you get a free meal at Denny's on your birthday. We could—"

"Just get the goddamn chew and bake a cake. White—with white frosting."

"I like chocolate."

"Course you do. If I'd a said chocolate, you'd want white."

"It's my birthday. I oughta have the kind a cake *I* like. I oughta have friends and a present from my husband."

"You know where the gate is if you don't like it."

"If I had somewhere to go, I'd go."

"Why don't you track down your worthless son. Let him take care a you."

"You're the reason Joey left," Ruth mumbled, knowing Ray couldn't hear, and swallowed the lump in her throat. Joey had taken Ray's constant criticism for years, but the day it become physical, he'd left and Ruth hadn't seen him since. Her eyes stung as she stared at the cold, runny egg on her plate. Blinking back tears, she reached under the table and pinched her forearm as hard as she could, and under that gray sweater, little bruises freckled her arm.

"Hey, I know!" Ray startled her. "Better yet, go live with your druggie daughter. Probably back in jail."

"Jail's gotta be better than livin' with you." She said it loud so he could hear.

Ray stood and Ruth looked down. When he went to the fridge and chugged milk from the carton, Ruth cleared his plate and took it to the sink. "Whorin' around with niggers, takin' drugs. Blame me all you want—*ain't* my fault Jessica's useless. Hell, she probably got herself killed a long time ago anyway."

Ruth turned and faced him. "You're a pig. A heartless, pathetic pig."

"And you're a worthless cunt." His cruelty had lost its sting so long ago that it allowed space for an idea to bud, then bloom. Her refusal to waste one more moment forced an epiphany. It was perfection. Maybe God had been watching and bestowed upon her the flawless ploy. Atonement gave Ruth all the courage she needed.

"Not today." She marched to the bedroom.

The double-barreled shotgun was wedged between Ray's side of the bed and the nightstand. Ruth cracked open the breech; a shell filled each chamber. The old gun stuck twice before Ruth forced it shut and walked out with it at her waist.

Ray was planted on the pot when Ruth came into the bathroom, shotgun cradled in her arms. "What the hell you doin'?" His dirty britches gathered at his boots—a *Western Horseman* magazine open on his lap.

11

"Give me the keys to the truck." Ruth held out her hand. The gun followed.

"You're crazy."

"I'm leavin' you, Ray. Give me the keys."

"Ruth, darlin', what's got you all twisted up?" Ray's smile was unconvincing. "Come on, we'll go to Lenny's and—" Ray grabbed for the gun but missed. Ruth recoiled; she didn't mean to jerk the trigger. Pieces of ceiling fell like hail as Ray dove into a fetal position on the floor. "Jesus Christ, woman!"

"Give me the dang keys, Raymond!"

Ray squirmed on the floor and pulled up his pants. He fought his pocket to find the keys, then held them out. She snatched them. The mix of adrenaline and satisfaction caused something as close to ecstasy as Ruth could remember. A laugh emerged from deep inside that would not be contained.

Melting snow wept from the tin roof. A dark cloud of spent diesel purged from the tailpipe as the old Dodge fishtailed up the snowy drive and out the front gate. Ruth followed the plow truck until snow turned to rain. The gas gauge hit *E* after half an hour, but Ruth reached San Andreas. Tommy's Bakery caught her eye. She had always wanted one of those fancy coffees, but Ray didn't approve of doing business with queers. Ruth parked the truck and walked in.

The air was a delicious mix of warm vanilla and coffee beans. A young man with a creamy complexion slid a tray of cinnamon rolls into the display case, then popped out and smiled. "Well, good morning. What can I get you?"

"Got any chocolate birthday cakes?"

"No, so sorry. Let's order one, shall we? Have it by tomorrow."

"That's okay." Ruth inspected the fruit-glazed tarts, the pies, muffins, scones, and sophisticated-looking pastries of all sorts.

"So, *whose* birthday?"

"Mine."

"Oh! Happy birthday. Let me guess. Fifty—fifty-one?"

"Haaa!" Ruth liked this guy even though she knew he was just being polite. "I'm seventy . . . plus five."

"Well, you look absolutely fantastic, let me tell you." The guy clasped his hands and held them at his chin. "Do you like tortes?"

"I—don't know."

"I have a fabulous chocolate torte that someone ordered. Someone I'm not very fond of, unprofessional, I know, but, whatever, I could"—he looked around as if someone would hear his secret—"let you have it and make another one." He pressed his finger against his lips. "Shhh."

"It's not that important."

"Are you kidding me? It's your birthday. Ma'am, if you are really seventy-five and have yet to experience a chocolate torte, it is my duty—no, my honor—to serve you. My tortes are *amazing*." He opened a stainless-steel refrigerator, pulled out a triple-layer chocolate torte. Baby-blue and lavender-colored pansies planted along the top and bottom reminded Ruth of the small bouquet Ray had brought her when they married at the courthouse.

"Oh my gosh." She had never seen a more magnificent cake. Probably expensive, though. "What sort of fancy coffee would go with it?" Ruth bit her smile.

Customers crowded into line as Ruth sat at a corner table, sipped her cappuccino, and watched young, normal, happy people with their entire lives ahead of them. Without looking up, they knew which drinks to order while thumbing their phones. Knew how to live in a world where neighbors smiled and waved; didn't threaten to call the sheriff because your cattle busted through the fence. They lived with pets who were allowed in the house, who served no purpose other than companionship. Their world had family and friends and birthday parties.

Ruth finished her extra-large slice of torte, letting the last bite linger. The smooth chocolate coated her tongue, and she washed it down with the last of her cappuccino. Like a cow working a salt block, Ruth licked her fork clean, then slid it into her coat pocket. A pink box held the remaining torte, and Ruth took a long last look before closing the lid.

The old Dodge rolled to a stop in front of Wells Fargo. It coughed and farted when Ruth killed the engine. She grabbed the shotgun off the floorboard and unloaded it, her heart throbbed in her chest as she stared out the fogged windshield. Shadows of cars passed every so often, and Ruth caught herself wondering where they all were going. She was putting it off and thought about going home. In less than a moment, Ruth took the gun and the pink box into the bank.

"Hi, Ruth!" Helen, who worked at the Mountain Ranch post office, was filling out a deposit slip.

"Hi, Helen. How are you?" Ruth smiled and set the pink box on the counter.

"Great. How are—" She noticed the gun.

Ruth raised the gun and stepped up to the only teller. A redheaded girl, still battling acne, smiled disbelievingly. "Hey, Mrs. Peterson."

"Hi, Amber. I'm sorry, sweetie, but can I please have *all* your money? I'm robbing the bank. Okay?"

Amber dropped her chin and raised her brow before she opened her drawer. "What am I supposed to put it in?"

Ruth hadn't considered details. Fear quickly fogged her mind. Her heart began to beat impossibly loud in her ears and caused her hands and legs to tremble. Light-headed and unstable, she felt like she might buckle at any moment. Everything told her to sit down, tell Amber she was "sorry" and "never mind, it was only a joke." But it was now or back to Ray. "Find something!" It felt good to yell. She grabbed a deep breath and watched Amber remove the plastic bag from a trash can. "Good thinkin'."

Amber filled the bag with cash from the drawer and handed it to Ruth as the new branch manager, a woman in her forties and a navy suit-dress, ducked behind a desk.

"Thank you. Now go press the alarm or whatever you're supposed to do." Ruth used the unloaded gun like a cane, hugged the pink box with the cash riding on top, and took a seat in the waiting area. Soft jazz played while the new manager, and Amber, and especially Helen, watched Ruth dig the fork out of her coat pocket and eat her birthday torte.

"Ruth? What in the *world* are you *doing*?" Helen

15

asked from across the room.

"Leaving Ray."

It seemed like forever for the Sheriff's Department to arrive, but when they did, they came in full force. Six of them in flak jackets with assault rifles scanned the area for the bandit. The manager pointed to Ruth. With the fork in her hand, Ruth raised her arms like she'd seen the bad guys do on reruns of *Magnum, P.I.*

"Drop the weapon!"

Ruth dropped her fork.

"Stand up and place your hands on your head!" a voice from behind her roared. Ruth stood, did as she was told, and her chair flew sideways. Strong hands expertly pinioned her arms behind her back. The cold cuffs were on in an instant, and Ruth grinned all the way to the police car. She grinned while being fingerprinted. Even grinned in her booking photo.

Judge Amy Jackson leaned forward on the bench at Ruth Peterson's arraignment. "Considering the severity of the charges, this is a difficult case. The defendant lacks any criminal history."

"'Cause she ain't no criminal, Judge. Just let her come home. I need her . . . I'm starvin' to death." Ray stood behind Ruth and patted her shoulder.

Judge Jackson slammed her gavel twice. "Mr. Peterson! You must refrain from speaking. I've warned you, these outbursts will not be tolerated—next time, I will have you removed and fined, do you understand?"

Ray twisted his ball cap in his hands. "I think freedom of speech is still my right as an American, ain't it?"

"Get him out of here," Judge Jackson ordered.

Ruth and her sweaty public defender, David Mendoza, watched as the bailiff and the security guard escorted Ray out the heavy doors.

"Your Honor, my client pleads guilty to all charges and wishes to refuse bail." Mendoza's statement sounded more like a question.

"Considering the special circumstances of this case, I find the bail schedule to be excessive. The fact that the defendant failed to remove the money from the bank's premises also challenges the robbery charge. Until I can further review and determine the specifics pertaining to this case, I am ordering the defendant to house arrest."

"What? What did she say?" Panic filled Ruth.

"You get to go home, Mrs. Peterson." Mendoza patted Ruth's shoulder.

"No!" Ruth shook her head. "I don't want to go home."

Ruth had been home two days before she shared secrets with the mounted deer head next to the woodstove whenever Ray was near. "Don't worry, I won't tell him," she'd say. "Wait 'til he goes to sleep, then we'll get him," she'd whisper loudly so Ray could hear. Then she'd cover her mouth and giggle. By the fourth day, Ray put the deer head in the shed. He hid his collection of hunting knives that once decorated the living room, and the shotgun was no longer loaded or next to the bed.

At dinner, Ruth set a casserole dish on the table and folded her hands in prayer. Ray ignored her and lifted the lid. Steam off the olive-colored meatballs caused him to gag. There was no mistaking the smell of horse manure.

17

"You goddamn lunatic! I'm callin' that probation fella."

Ruth rushed to the refrigerator, pulled Probation Officer Joshua Nelson's card off the door, and handed it to Ray.

By noon the next day, Probation Officer Joshua Nelson sat at the kitchen table and watched Ruth peel two bananas with her mouth. She held one in each hand.

"Last night, I woke up—she's standin' over me with a goddamn butcher knife singing 'Happy Birthday.'" Ray crossed his arms and leaned back against his chair.

"Has she seen a doctor?" Joshua asked as Ruth bit each banana.

"No." Ray eyed Ruth while she filled her mouth and cheeks.

Joshua wrote on a tablet in his file folder. "We should start with a basic examination followed by—" Ruth spit the entire mouthful of banana on Ray's face.

"Ruth!" Ray grabbed her hands. The mess crept down his face as if he were melting and justified Ruth's laughing frenzy.

"You're gonna make me pee my pants!" Ruth hurried to the bathroom. Pulled her pants down without closing the door.

"I'll order an immediate evaluation," said Joshua.

"Evaluate this." Ruth squatted and peed on the floor.

Ray leaned sideways in his chair and watched Ruth repeat, "I'm not cleanin' it up. I'm not cleanin' it up."

"She's pissin' on the goddamn floor!" Ray stood, arms akimbo, and eyed Joshua. "She's fucking nuts."

"I'll call someone," Joshua delivered in a somber voice.

Not answering even one of the evaluation questions caused the county to label Ruth incoherent. The second series of evaluations identified her behavior as dementia. Taking her home was not advised.

Paradise Ranch Senior Care gave Ruth her own room and an extra-large flat-screen high-definition television with channels galore. They cleaned her bathroom twice a week, organized yoga, and bingo, and polka night. After a month, Ruth had over a dozen friends. One in particular, Charlie, saved the chocolates his daughter brought and shared them with Ruth.

"Charlie." Ruth loved saying his name. Loved the way it sounded. *Charlie.* Loved the way his luminous gray-green eyes listened when she spoke as if her words mattered. Loved his gravelly voice when he read and explained D. H. Lawrence poems. Loved the minty smell of his brown skin.

It was April Fool's Day when Ray visited. "Heifers did good, not much trouble this year." He sat on the edge of a chair in the corner of Ruth's room and watched her work the fancy TV remote from her upright bed. She paused on the Superior Livestock Auction taking place in Nebraska. "What is this?" Ray perked up and watched the cattle being sold. "That herd don't average no eight hundred pounds. Turn it up," he ordered. Ruth changed the channel to Oprah, tried to ignore the odor of cow manure that always festered on Ray. "Turn that back right now." His chest and shoulders swelled.

Ruth turned up the volume. "Hush. I'm watchin' Oprah."

Ray snatched the remote from Ruth. She laughed

when he pressed the on-off button three times. "How the hell you work this damn thing?"

"You have to be nice to it." Ruth knew he couldn't see the buttons because he was too stubborn to wear glasses.

"Well, I come to visit you." Ray tossed her the remote. "Try and *remember that*."

"Remember? I don't remember you." Ruth looked confused. "Who are you?"

Ray bent close to Ruth's face. "You know goddamn well who I am. You ain't foolin' me one damn bit."

"I don't have to," Ruth said. And she never spoke to him again. Not one word when he visited twice in May.

In June, Ray found Ruth outside at a picnic table, sitting too close to Charlie. They worked a jigsaw puzzle under the shade of cedar trees. With a handful of wildflowers, Ray stomped up in a crisp white button-down and new jeans. "Guess we can figure why your daughter likes them colored boys, huh?" He spit a stream of tobacco juice. Tried to rile Charlie with a long, threatening glare. When Charlie high-fived Ruth for placing the last puzzle piece, Ray threw the flowers at them and left.

February felt like spring. Charlie knocked on Ruth's door just before noon. She sat on her bed, reading *The Complete Poems of D. H. Lawrence.* He left the door open and sat on the bed next to her. "Happy birthday, Ruth." He smiled like he meant it and handed her a box wrapped in gleaming gold paper.

"What did you do?" Ruth held the gift, admired it a long while. "It's so beautiful." A warmth washed over

her. "Probably the most beautiful thing I've ever seen."
She didn't fight the lump in her throat or the happy
tears when they came.

"Come on now—none of that." Charlie put his arm
around her. "Open it up, Ruthie, lunch is getting cold."
He pulled her in close and didn't look away when he
wiped her tears.

"Thank you, Charlie." She would have been satisfied
to sit on that bed with Charlie for the rest of the day.
Maybe the rest of her life.

"Please open the present. I can smell the lasagna.
I'm hungry."

"Okay, okay." Ruth removed the tape and
unwrapped the box without ripping the paper. She
wiggled the lid off. "What the heck is it?"

"It's an iPad. They're wonderful. You can take
pictures, check the weather, watch videos. You can even
download all the books or poems you like. I'll show
you later."

Ruth filled her lungs, felt them expand, felt the
privilege of just being alive. Then, in the space of a
heartbeat, she wrapped her arms around Charlie's neck.
Their kiss was simple, soft and slow, but most of all, it
was sincere. Something Ruth had forgotten she needed.
The appreciation of how enjoyable life had become in
only a year of trying was not lost on her.

"That was nice." Charlie leaned in and kissed Ruth
again. "I've wanted to kiss you since you got here."

Ruth giggled and blushed like a schoolgirl.

"I'd like to kiss you again after lunch. *If* that's okay
with you?"

Ruth nodded. "Yes."

Charlie was all smiles when he took Ruth's hand and hurried her down the hall.

"Shhh, here she comes. Quiet everyone." Hushed voices escaped from the cafeteria.

ANGELS CAMP

A banner struggles to escape its tethers above the dark entrance. *Welcome to Calaveras County Fair and Jumping Frog Jubilee.* Colossal cement frogs flank the muddy road, grinning as headlights hit them. Remnants of cotton candy linger, as does the chill of a May night. Rows of American flag pennants snap and salute rodeo fans as they exit across a soggy pasture parking lot. Under a full moon, Gene Autry crackles "Happy Trails" through rusty speakers.

Behind the bucking chutes, Joe Quick, a lanky bullfighter ten years past his prime, pries a black Resistol off his dirty-blond head. Dried sweat crusts his red-white-and-blue clown cheeks as he limps by a dozen portable pens restraining bucking bulls and broncs. Popcorn mingles with manure. Joe stops. Looks at Spooky, voted bucking bull of the year. The massive black bull smacks his head against the metal rails and keeps it there until Joe rubs and scratches the sweet spot just below and between his banana horns.

"Are you the rodeo clown?"

Joe turns to see a girl missing her front teeth but

smiling like she hasn't a care in the world. "I'm a bullfighter—not a clown. I save guys from getting hammered by a bull."

"What about girls? Do you save them too?" Her stringy brown hair flaps like wings under her cowboy hat.

"I would—just ain't that many girl bull riders around. I'm Joe. What's your name?" Joe holds out his hand.

"Chyann. I'm gonna be a bull rider. Or . . . maybe, a bullfighter like you." The girl pulls a marker from her back pocket. "Will you autograph my hat?"

"I'd be honored." Joe signs his name across the back brim and dumps the girl's hat back on her head.

"Thank you!" Chyann runs to her parents as they give Joe a wave of appreciation.

In the door of his flatbed, Joe finds his OxyContin and downs them with a perspiring can of Coors. A cell phone on the seat dings, and Joe grabs it: 10:15. He listens to the message from his wife. "Hi, hon. I'm going to bed, so don't call. That paint colt finally launched me like a lawn dart today. Counterfeit bugger even tried to kick me while I was down. Anyhoo, don't worry, I'm fine, just tired. Hurry up and get your butt home. I took rib eyes out for dinner tomorrow. Love ya."

"Love you too," Joe whispers and tosses the phone on the seat.

"Good work tonight." A corn-fed old cowboy rides toward Joe.

"Thanks, boss." Joe scrapes makeup from his cheeks with a dirty rag and looks in his side mirror. "Can you pay me in cash?"

"Pay you?" It sounds more like a statement than a question. "Your pay's goin' toward what you owe me."

Joe stops scraping. "Can I get half?"

"Soon as I do."

Joe looks up with a smeared smile. "Me and Em's tryin' real hard to build a cabin."

"Keep tryin'." Boss spits a long stream of tobacco juice as he rides away.

Roper struts up looking like a young Elvis. "Dang! Boss Hog be gettin' fat as a tick on a tampon!"

Joe knocks back his beer and comes up for air. "You get the money?" He crawls onto the flatbed.

"Don't *even* get me started. Last night, at the dance, me and this biker dude, we totally hit it off right. *Really* hit it off." A sigh causes Roper's smile to stray. "After dinner, we sinned, and, you know. Long story short, I fell asleep and the fag stole my money." He unzips his Wranglers. "Does this look infected?" Digging in his underwear, Roper faces Joe. "No, seriously, look. Do I need *penis*-cillin?" Roper's laugh is more like a bray.

"Get back, just—if you ain't got the cash—" Joe can't avoid looking in Roper's direction. Peeking from his zipper is a roll of cash.

"Ha! I knew you'd look. Perv!"

Joe shakes his head and grins. "You fucking need therapy."

"Nope, hanging around a loser like you makes me feel much better about myself. These undies are cool, right?" Roper works the wad of bills back into the Velcro money pocket. "Found them online. I can get you a pair?" He zips up as Joe slides off the flatbed. "Got *your* money, honey?" Roper asks, crossing his

25

arms.

"Yeah, but I had to earn mine, you trust fund bitch." Joe grabs a denim shirt from inside the cab.

"Don't be hatin'. I'm broke as you are. Had to borrow money from Auntie."

An aching pain punches through Joe as he removes his Red Bull jersey, revealing a scar the size of a silver dollar below his sternum. A souvenir from Bushwacker—a bull that killed one rider and caused another to think like a third-grader. A horn had impaled Joe as he worked at freeing a rider's hand wedged in the bull rope. Saving the cowboy cost Joe two weeks in ICU and a season without pay. A fundraiser paid the bills for three months. Bankruptcy covered the rest.

"Let's go over this again, just in case. I can*not* lose this money. Bankruptcy is not an option for people with trust funds." Roper dips his hands into his jean pockets.

"Fuck you." Joe eyes Roper.

"I didn't mean because you filed—I just . . . forget it. Regular old five-card draw, right?"

"Maybe you shouldn't come with me." Joe closes only one of the three pearl snaps on his right cuff, leaving the two nearest his palm undone. "This ain't the game for beginners."

"I know how to play poker. Winner take all, right?" Roper pulls a new deck from his shirt pocket. "Hey, what if their cards are different than ours?"

"This ain't my first rodeo. In a few hours, that wad won't fit in your panties." Joe snags the deck from Roper, slides the cards out, and fans them like a sophisticated street magician. "Handkerchief?"

Roper pops a white hanky from his vest pocket like a well-trained assistant. Gene Autry concludes "Happy

Trails," and the night goes silent.

Joe folds two aces into the handkerchief and tucks it into his shirt pocket. He sneezes, pulls the handkerchief out and wipes his nose, then stuffs it back into his shirt pocket. Voila, the two aces are gone. Sliding his sleeve up, Joe exposes the cards. Bouncing like an excited pup, Roper claps. "Amen! I love you! I'm gonna enter every Podunk rodeo in the West."

"Me and Em have to start the cabin or I'm in deep shit." The arena lights pop off. "*Wooo*" and "*Yeeowww*" echo from drunk fans desperate for fun.

Angels Camp is a refurbished gold rush town complete with mercantile, three-story hotel, and corner saloon with a former brothel upstairs. Hanging from a clothesline above the deserted street, antique dresses, worn-out overalls, and torn flannel shirts float like ghosts. Vintage lamps line Main Street as frogs harmonize with Roper's spurs—clicking and clacking and croaking.

"Why the hell didn't you take your spurs off?" Joe asks.

"I forgot, okay?" Roper steps around painted frogs on the sidewalk. "Don't have a tizzy. Not like I flimflam people every day. I'm usually extremely ethical. I believe that—"

"Rope! It's fine."

They pass Utica Park—named for the Utica gold mine—burial site of seventeen men who perished when it collapsed. Entombed below a slide and row of swings. A bronze statue of Mark Twain glares down at them as they pass. Sprinklers kick on, hissing until they reach the dark end of Main Street. "You cannot fuck

27

this up. Understand? Not one of these fuckers wants to lose at a winner-take-all game. Tell me again why this works," says Joe.

Balling his fists, Roper walks faster and faster. "Okay, okay . . . When the cards come to you for the third time, everyone will have a hand they *think* they can win with. They'll bet big. We do too. You sneeze—pull your hanky, slip the aces in, and we win."

Made of century-old pine and washed in white, Saint Joseph's church waits like a savior. Saint Financial Aid. Below the oxidized brass bell, a Roman-numeral clock reads midnight.

"Midnight mass. Last time I played with this gangbanger from Stockton. Father Ortega asked the dude if he'd been baptized. I don't know if the guy didn't hear him or what. But ole Ortega had one ear off and was whittlin' at the other before the bastard could even get up and run. Mexicans didn't touch him, that's how connected he is. He killed his brother for cheatin' on his wife—I heard he keeps him in the freezer and hacks off chunks to put in the beans."

"OMG." Roper comes to a halt. "He'll hate me, right?"

"Fuck yeah. Don't talk. Don't make eye contact. Just sit the fuck down and look at your cards." Joe gives the handkerchief in his shirt a final adjustment.

Darkness cloaks the rear of the church as Joe approaches a skinny back door. "Shit. He'll lock this. If *anything* goes wrong, you hit this door and you hit it hard as you can. It'll bust, and you run, keep running, don't look back no matter what." The old door bleats like a sacrificial lamb as Joe opens it. Roper follows.

Down warped and narrow steps that lead to a dim glow. Creaking wood and clapping spurs amplify each step as the wail of an organ begins.

"This is all kinds of creepy, man." Roper puts his hand on Joe's shoulder. "Smells like something's burning."

"Simmering flesh—now shut the fuck up."

The organ trembles as they enter the dank basement. Burning votives and Virgin Mary veladoras crowd the cramped space, along with a folding hexagonal card table and three strangers. Father Ortega stands in a black floor-length cassock accented with a shoulder cape. At six-foot-five, he is an effigy of something sinister and looks down upon them with dark, wilting eyes. Roper grabs Joe's arm and squeezes.

"Donations?" Father Ortega's authoritative voice commands, his gnarled hands holding out a donation basket. Roper attempts to ignore the chains tattooed around Ortega's wrists, the Glock holstered under his arm, but an inappropriate laugh escapes.

Joe pulls a white envelope from his back pocket, _IN GOD WE TRUST_ written across the front in blue clown eyeliner. He places it in the basket.

Roper palms the wad of cash in his secret underwear. Looks up at the priest. "Is the bathroom, is, umm, there a bathroom?"

Ortega's razor-burnt chin clenches into his neck like a closing fist. Nostrils flare. The heavy cassock swings as Ortega seems to float across the room. Stopping at the freezer, he sets the basket down. With a swift slap, Ortega stifles the organ music coming from a cassette player and roars, "And he shall lay his hand upon the head of his offering and *kill it* at the door of the tabernacle of the congregation!" He takes a calming breath and softens. "Leviticus."

Roper turns away, digging out his cash as fast as he can. Delicately, he lays ten thousand dollars in the donation basket. With eyes locked on Roper, Ortega flips through the curling bills like they're pages of a Bible.

At the card table, Joe sits between a bearded Brit and Luke, who wears a grizzled Afro and huge sunglasses. Miss Kitty takes the seat across from Joe. A pucker-faced woman in blue eye shadow and a lacquered auburn twist taps her long gold nails like claws practicing for a concerto. Ortega blesses Roper with the sign of the cross. "May the Lord be with you."

"Thank you. Thank you very much. You too, sir, Father." Roper stumbles into the seat next to Miss Kitty.

Ortega drops the deck in front of Roper. "Shuffle." He flips the cassette over, and organ music grinds as Roper shuffles. Miss Kitty lights a long brown cigarette and takes a deep drag while Ortega divides poker chips between players. "Ladies first." Ortega slides the deck to Miss Kitty. "I will watch over my flock." He raises his palms above his head and explodes, "And I will inflict the wrath of God upon the sinners!" Roper squirms in his chair as Miss Kitty deals the first hand.

By two a.m. smoke clouds the basement and a dozen brown cigarette butts litter a silver tray. Miss Kitty lights another as Joe sniffs and wipes his nose on his sleeve. Poker chips applaud as the Brit drags in another winning pile.

"Beans are ready." Ortega waits for a response. No one looks up. No one responds. Luke rubs under his glasses and pushes the deck to Joe. Joe sniffs, shuffles, and sniffs again as Ortega watches. "Coming down with something, my son?"

"Allergies. Happens every spring." Joe wipes his nose with his sleeve again and deals. The organ quits and Joe swallows hard. The Brit, smiling with everything except his lips, stares wide-eyed at his hand. Miss Kitty taps her nails a beat faster, and Luke remains cool behind his shades. Roper sneaks a peek at Ortega, who is now glaring at Joe.

"Would you like a tissue?" Ortega grins.

"Sure." Joe adjusts the cards in his hand.

Ortega rises—moves next to Joe. Leans in uncomfortably close. "Why?"

"Why what, Father?" Joe avoids eye contact.

Ortega jacks his gun and shoves it against Joe's nose. "Why go to all the trouble of carrying such a nice handkerchief and not make use of it?"

"I forgot I had the damn thing!" Joe tightens his brow and shuts his eyes.

"Well, then, give it a whirl, won't you?" Ortega insists.

The moment lingers before anyone moves, or speaks, or breathes. Roper's palms press against the green felt table as Joe draws the handkerchief slowly—carefully—from his shirt and dabs his nose, then replaces it. Miss Kitty reaches across the table and snatches the handkerchief—freeing the aces to buck wildly through the air and land on the table. Joe shoves himself into Ortega and flips the table. "Run!"

Gunfire explodes. Screaming, Roper lunges for the

31

stairs. Ears ringing, they take the steps two at a time, unable to escape the sour acrid smell of spent gunpowder. "Go, go, go!" Joe's muffled panic repeats. "Go!"

At the top of the stairs, Roper catapults himself through the locked door. Fragile wood cracks and antique hinges give. Another shot as Roper and the door crash against the gravel lot. Two more shots burst from the basement. Joe grabs Roper's arm and drags him across the lot then down an embankment. They drop into the creek behind the church.

"Move your ass!"

For a quarter mile, they splash between boulders and branches. Spiderwebs sticking. Swatting. Squealing. Stumbling over slick stones, Roper goes down. "Shit!"

"Come on! Up here." Joe cuts out of the creek. Up a steep bank on all fours. A barbwire fence stops them. Stepping on the bottom strand and pulling up on the next, Joe stretches the middle section of the fence wide open. "Hurry." Roper wiggles through, then reciprocates the process. Joe slips between the wires like a snake between stacked brush. They sprint under a full moon. Casting long demonic shadows across an overgrazed pasture—closing in on a dilapidated barn.

Weathered wood offers sanctuary. Joe steps through a missing plank, but Roper struggles. No tools, no tractor, no bales of hay, only fermenting earth, creosote, and feces stagnate the empty space. Joe sucks air through his open mouth as Roper heaves in the corner. "I—I kinda pooped my pants."

Joe laughs with lungs deprived of oxygen. He can't stop laughing, then doubles over holding his side.

"*So* not funny." Roper tugs and tugs until his wet boots and spurs release.

Joe's hysterics go on and on until, finally, a long silence fills the open space. "I promised Em I wouldn't play cards no more. She finds out I been gamblin' . . . lost this much money—she'll kill me." Joe puts his hand on Roper's shoulder. ".38 in my truck will fix this shit right now."

"Nope! *Not even* going back! Donation to staying alive! You don't get caught cheating and expect to get your money back. Not with that creepazoid. Oh God, do they know where you live?"

"They think I'm from Lodi. And run a vineyard there."

"We are so lucky." Roper plops onto the dirt floor. "Maybe I can write it off. What do I tell Auntie?"

"I'm fucked. I borrowed that cash from a guy in Vegas!" Joe blows a long breath and sits next to Roper.

"I'd float you a loan, but I don't get another check until fall."

"Sorry, Rope. Really. Sorry you ruined your fancy underwear."

"It's not your fault." Roper unbuckles his belt. "I'd probably be dead if it weren't for you." He wiggles out of his soggy jeans. "You always got my back . . . I want you to know I appreciate it." He slides out of the secret-pocket undies.

Joe throws his hat against the ground and lies on his back. Clasps his arms over his forehead and stares at the speckled sky through the broken roof. "I'm such a fucking asshole."

"Yes, you are. But Em loves you, and so do I." Roper wipes and tosses the soiled undies into the corner. "She won't stop just 'cause you can't build the cabin"—he wiggles his legs into his jeans—"so you have to stay in the trailer a while longer—so what. It's not the end of the world."

"We could a been killed. Or shot." Joe grins and shakes his head. "Or worse . . . you fucking floppin' around the ER flirtin' with the doctor like last time."

Roper looks down at Joe and grins. "Amen, brother."

Sunday morning blossoms as church bells echo down Main Street. Joe climbs the blue steps of the white church that offers benevolence in the light of day. Sliding into the last pew, Joe sits next to a weathered man in jeans and a tan canvas coat. The faithful flock sit upfront.

Playing "Ave Maria" on the organ, Miss Kitty, in her Sunday best, sings and smiles at Joe. The weathered man slides closer. Pulls the _IN GOD WE TRUST_ envelope from his coat pocket and hands it to Joe with the same gnarled fingers and tattooed wrists of Father Ortega.

"Took three hundred from your cut. Have to pay my cousin for the door, and everyone said you should have left it unlocked. That cool?" The soft words sound nothing like the Father Ortega from last night.

Joe holds the envelope down near his knees and opens it. Without removing the one-hundred-dollar bills, he carefully counts his share. Finally, when he reaches seventy-seven, he closes the envelope. Folds it in half and tucks it deep into the inside pocket of his leather jacket.

"Thanks, Abe." Joe stands.

"You're not staying for the service?"

"Em's waitin'. Gotta get home." Joe pats Abe on the shoulder and the music stops.

"I'll pray for you."

Joe slips his hands in his jacket pockets and caresses the cash inside. His boots echo like flesh slapping hardwood. Out the door. Down the steps.

CALAVERAS

Johnny Cash plays through a dust-covered boom box, rattling the barn's tin roof. Unashamed of her incompetent pitch, Emma Lee sings too loud while loading the last shovelful of horse manure into a wheelbarrow. She leans the shovel against the log wall and sings, "Bound by wild desire—I fell into a ring of fire." With a quick pull, she tightens her tawny bobbed ponytail. Unsophisticated and wholesome, she's just short of beautiful. Twenty-eight years ago, Emma Lee Dunnigan was accidentally born in this barn, a story her mother loves repeating whenever Emma Lee leaves a door open. Muscles on her rangy arms strain under her Lynyrd Skynyrd tee as she fights the ornery wheelbarrow—pushing it along a dirt trail behind the barn. Hank, a decrepit border collie, and Huck, her year-old brindle rescue pup, follow.

The ranch is graced with seasonal creeks that grumble in spring—threading their way down acres of jade-colored hills, through a lush meadow, until finally reaching an impressive pond. Apple trees are heavy with soft pink petals that flutter and fall. That bold, sweet scent after a spring rain induces a sudden and inexplicable optimism. Cows watch their calves buck and play in pastures where spicy cedars and pines reach for the sky. Ancient oaks cast twisted shadows.

"Em?" Kate, a graying and wilting version of Em, shouts as she untangles herself from clean white sheets hanging on the clothesline behind her clean white house. "Made a pot of spaghetti."

"No, thanks, Mom. Joe's comin' home. Gonna cook him a steak," Em yells from the barn as she drops the empty wheelbarrow.

Cramped in the Airstream, Em washes her hands and face in a miniature bathroom sink. Nails chewed to the quick. A blast of deodorant under each arm. A dab of mascara, then peach lip gloss tidies her appearance. Overhead, a mischievous fly drones. She swats twice at the pest, then scrutinizes herself in the mirror duct-taped above the sink. Letting her hair down, she combs it to the side and considers it. Too boyish. She parts it down the middle, hoping for something trendy, then wraps the sides behind her ears, grunts, and pulls it back into a ponytail. The droning stops as the fly lands on the mirror and is exterminated with a smack. A wing, and specks of red and fluorescent yellow, smear Em's hand. The dismembered carcass lands on a pregnancy test stick resting on the counter.

Joe's Ford purrs up to the trailer, and Em bolts out the door, wiping wet hands on dirty jeans. She married Joe Quick four years ago during the National Finals Rodeo in Las Vegas. The previous year, Joe had fought bulls and Emma Lee was Miss Rodeo California. Reluctantly, she primped and competed for the title of

Miss Rodeo America. The winning queen would receive a twenty-thousand-dollar scholarship and give Em her shot at becoming a veterinarian. She won the horsemanship section of the competition, and an engraved silver buckle trimmed in imitation gold. The tarnished buckle sits next door, in her mom's house, on a shelf above the woodstove, covered in dust and ash, alongside two dozen others. Emma Lee finished third in the Miss Rodeo America competition and abandoned the pursuit of becoming a veterinarian in exchange for Joe, an Airstream on her mother's ranch, and part-time work as a vet tech at the Mother Lode Equine Clinic.

Joe kills the engine, climbs out of the truck as Em runs through dust and diesel fumes to him. Their attraction is magnetic—they fit together as if created that way. Joe cradles his wife's face in his hands, then smiles and tosses her over his shoulder like a sack of grain. "You got some ridin' to do, cowgirl." Up the Airstream steps, he attempts to squeeze through the narrow trailer door.

"Put me down! Really. I'm not kidding, Joe! You're squishin' him."

Joe stops. Backs off the steps, then slowly sets Em down. "Him?"

"I was gonna tell you after dinner."

His hazel eyes absorb her words. "I did it?"

"Yep." Em nods with an embarrassed grin, looks down, realizing her feet are bare.

"When? How pregnant are ya?"

"I'm thinking a few months, maybe. I missed my last two periods and—"

"You know it's a boy? For sure?"

"Got a feelin'."

"I gotta feelin' too. Feelin' our boy's gonna have his own room." Joe reaches into his back pocket and hands Em the *IN GOD WE TRUST* envelope.

She looks inside. Sees the cash. "What's this?"

"Down payment on the cabin."

"You been playin' cards? Tell the truth."

"It's the money Harvey owed me for driving the water truck on the Butte Fire. I ran into him after the rodeo."

An intense, almost-orgasmic pleasure surges through her, like sliding into a warm bath on a cold day. She leaps on Joe, cinches her arms around his neck, her legs tight around his waist. "I love you." She kisses his neck. Bites his earlobe. "I love you." Another kiss.

"Baby, I love you more. Holy shit, we're gonna have a baby!" He rocks her side to side.

Kate, with her long graying braid pulled to one side, yells as she approaches from the path between her house and the Airstream. "Forest Service called." A warm apple pie cradled in hands thickened by a lifetime of weather. "Hi, Joey."

Joe sets Em down and hugs his mother-in-law, who doesn't attempt to hug him back. She never has been a people person, and the pie in her hands prevents the usual awkwardness that comes with polite affection. "You're the best, Kate." A bouquet of warm apples and cinnamon linger as she hands him the pie.

"Forest Service said two of our cows are up on Devil's Nose. They didn't see no calves."

Em crosses her arms. "That's a three-hour ride if you hurry."

"I'll see if I can find where they busted through the fence." Joe scoops out a hunk of pie with his fingers.

"Go in the morning." Kate presses her thinning lips together.

"I'll take that paint colt. Be good for that dumb son of a bitch, 'specially if we're gonna brand calves next week?" Joe fills his mouth.

"We have to. And Roper asked if he could bring his sister. I said she could run the nut bucket." A grin lifts Kate's face. Savannah carrying a bucket of calf testicles seems somehow artistic.

"Perfect job for that skank," Joe says around a mouthful of pie.

"Be nice," Kate and Em recommend in unison, then look at each other until no one speaks. The silence thickens. Turns awkward as Kate tries to wait them out.

"So . . . ?" She rocks back on her heels. Looks at Em with tired but knowing brown eyes. "Anything else?"

Almost smiling, Em bites her lower lip—focusing on her bare feet. "Nope." She shrugs and shakes her head with the innocence of a guilty child.

Kate clasps her hands behind her back and waits another long minute. "Oh, come *on*, you two! Just 'cause I'm gonna be a gramma don't mean I'm deaf."

Like most nights, Kate eats dinner standing at the kitchen counter with old Hank, the dog, staring at his bowl. Waiting for leftovers. Only, tonight, Kate opens a bottle of Pinot she'd been saving for a special occasion. Wine works wonders on a woman's truth.
Grandmother. Grandma. Granny. None of them feels right. *Nana*? Hell no. Imagining being a grandparent brings a familiar mix of dread and optimism that came with the thought of ever dating. The dating was easy to excuse herself out of. It was always the same. *I can't*

make it. I have to fence to fix. You're welcome to come help? It culled the slackers. Kate gulps the last of her third glass of wine and sets it on the counter. Dumps her leftover spaghetti in Hank's bowl and watches him gulp it without chewing.

"Sorry I overcooked the steak." Em clears the plates off the collapsible table, the Airstream still filled with smoke to spite the open windows and door.

"It was good." Joe rubs his jaw as he chews and chews the last hunk of meat. "My mastication muscles were getting soft."

"What? Your masturbation muscles?" Em dumps the burnt meat onto one plate and sets it outside the door for Huck.

"I said *mastication.* I been savin' my masturbation muscle for you." Joe laughs, sweeping table crumbs into his hand.

"Good." Em leans against the sink. Smiles that sweet smile that she knows gets Joe every time. "I missed you."

"I missed you too." He's up and pressed against her. His hands gripping her ass, pulling her into him. "You're comin' with me to every rodeo from now on." His kisses are soft and short on her neck, then long and hard on her mouth. An overwhelming desire to feel his weight on top of her drives her to the couch. On her back, kicking off her flip-flops, Joe unzips her jeans. Kisses her stomach, then slides his tongue into her bellybutton. "Is it okay? I can't hurt the baby, right?"

"Don't flatter yourself." Em grins and arches as she wiggles out of her jeans.

41

"Holy shit, I love you." He seems surprised and undresses as if it were a timed event. "I mean it, Em, I fucking love you." His warmth inside her.

Fluorescent lights buzz and spill from the barn into the dark-blue dawn. A sorrel colt, cursed with white legs, eats at the feed manger as Joe pulls slack from leather straps and buckles down his bedroll—securing it behind his saddle. Heavy canvas saddlebags hang over the horse's flanks and stow enough provisions for two days. Perched on a shelf, above the tack room door, Joe stretches to reach a vintage aluminum tube, then forces it into the middle of his bedroll.

"You're takin' my dad's fly rod?" Em walks in, crossing her arms partly due to the cold but mostly due to the sentiment she has for her father's fly rod.

"Hey. Thought you wanted to sleep."

"Sleep when I get old." Em tests the tube's security with a twist and a push and a pull. "Suppose to be lookin' for cows, not trout."

"You're the best peanut-butter-and-jelly sandwich maker I know, but I need meat."

"Better bring some back for me and Mom."

"Yes, ma'am." After untying the colt, he kisses Em. "Love you." He bends and kisses her belly. "Love you too."

Outside the barn, Joe's ass hits the saddle a little too hard. The colt flings and drops his head. He bucks like an oil derrick—up and down and up and down as if in slow motion. Joe pulls one rein and tips the colt's nose—forcing him into a tight circle. After a half dozen circles, Joe kicks the horse and sends him hopping through the apple orchard. They lope toward the rising sun as Joe glances back at Em with a confident smile. Huck barks and takes the lead.

"Be careful!" She waves and whispers, "With that rod, you goofball."

Flies cling to the frosty Airstream. Wilting yellow tulips rise as the promise of warmth wakes them. The trailer door bursts open—thumps against metal. An explosion of vomit drowns the flowers as Em folds. Groans and catches her breath, then heaves again. Spewing every bit of beefy bile from her stomach. She spits and spits, then wipes her mouth with her vet tech smock. "God dang." After a long, deep breath, she takes a seat in the doorway, then looks at her watch. Already an hour late. Another long, slow drag of breath, and a bit of color returns to her cheeks. She digs the cell phone from her pocket and dials.

"Hey, Brandi, it's Em. Still at home—I'm sick. I don't think I can come in today. Thanks. Yeah, I'll see you tomorrow. Bye." She lies back on the cool doorway floor and rests her hand on her forehead. Long, deep breaths over and over until dogs bark at a speeding vehicle rumbling through the pine and down the gravel drive. A new heavy-duty Chevy slides to a stop, and Roper jumps out.

"Hey, Rope." Em stands, but he doesn't greet her with the extra-long hug he's been greeting her with since they wore braces and cutoffs with matching cowboy boots. He's trembling.

"Where's Joe?" With a hand on his hip, he looks away, shaking his head as tears bloom.

"Getting cows off Devil's Nose, what's wrong?"

43

"I loved that guy, looked up to him like a fucking brother."

Em grabs Roper's arm. "What is it?"

"You deserve better than that sick piece of shit." Roper swallows with tears in his voice. "It's Savannah."

Em pushes her fists deep into her smock pockets. Her shoulders rising. Tensing without permission.

"He's been messin' with my little baby sister! Jesus Christ—she's only fourteen!"

"I know how old she is."

Hiding his face in his hands, he cries like a girl, "When's he gonna be back?"

She stalls. Taking it in. Shakes her head. "How do you know this? For sure, I mean. 'Cause, you know, I hate to say it, but your sister isn't the most honest person." Her muted tone doesn't hide her desperation.

"I love you, Em—" Roper drops his hands from his face. "Savanah's pregnant!"

"Bullshit." Em stumbles backward into the trailer and slams the door.

"Fourteen, Em! Not cool. Not cool at all! And also illegal. My dad's reporting it to the sheriff. The fucker's going to jail unless I find him first." His voice seeps into the trailer through the open window. "He's corrupt, Em!"

No, he's not. Em sits on the edge of her bed—staring at a fly trying to escape a spiderweb. The back of her brain tingles with an intense itch that can't be scratched. As Roper's truck revs and tears away, a high-pitched buzz fractures Em's memory. Her vision blurs. She blinks. Faster and faster, then wipes her eyes with trembling fingers. Drags her palms down her face, again and again, wanting to clear the blur. Eyes shut tight, she finds the phone in her pocket and pulls it out.

Kate barges in. "Honey, Em, you okay?"

"You heard?" Em stands, but the overwhelming sensation of spinning sends her back down onto the bed.

"We'll figure this out." Kate forces calm as she squeezes Em's wrists.

"It's a lie. I know it. Why?" Em wipes her eyes. "Why is she doing this now?"

"Who knows. Just stay calm, and when Joe gets back—"

"He won't be back 'til tomorrow. He's gonna fish." Her heart is racing so hard it hurts. Her eyes sting. "What is wrong with Savannah? Roper's gone nuts. He said Joe's going to jail." Em scrubs her eyes with the base of her palms.

"Don't fool with your eyes, hon." *Goddamn it, don't start up with your eyes. Please.*

"Don't look," Em whispers—freeing her wrists. Scrubbing her eyes hard.

"Stop rubbin' your eyes! Listen to me—" Panic rising in Kate's voice.

"I should talk to Dad. I haven't even told him he's going to be a grandpa."

Kate's face collapses. Her rosy cheeks turn pale. "Honey, you *know* you can't do that."

"Out please." Em jumps up—forces Kate back, out the door, then locks it.

Flies that had clung to the outside of the trailer are alive and well and buzzing in Kate's face. With her back pressed against the locked door, panic fogs her thinking. She can't contemplate her next move.

Beeping tones of numbers being dialed on a cell sneak out the open slotted window. "Daddy, it's Em . . . I miss you too. Can you come home?" Em's warm words uncoil like a hissing snake. "You're gonna be a grandpa." Chills suck the air from Kate. She covers her mouth with both hands. Considers praying. It never helped before. Goddamn it. How has she reached middle age and knows less than she ever has?

Agony rushing her. Ripping the old wound wide open. The wound she thought Joe had healed. A strange invasion like rapid blood loss makes her weak. Shaking, she stumbles off the doorstep, then catches herself and sits. Reaching out for something to stabilize her. Reaching for something that isn't there. Quietly falling apart as she listens. "And . . . Joe. They're saying he did a real bad thing. I don't believe it, but Roper said he got Savannah pregnant. They're gonna arrest him!"

Fraught with Em's long silence, Kate waits, still as a bird in a bush.

"Devil's Nose. We had some cows run off, and he went to get 'em." Kate doesn't breathe. A cold, dark terror passes through her like the sun just turned black.

Neon pinks, violets, and blues light the back of Devil's Nose as darkness devours the day. In the meadow below, Joe's colt's front legs are bound by a set of burlap hobbles tied above his ankles. A mound of tender new grass tempts the colt. He stumbles forward and tears a mouthful. Campfire embers flitter up a wall of quaking aspen as Joe tosses in another log. Green cedar pops and hisses as Joe stares into the dancing flames. A twig snaps somewhere in the brush and rattles his senses. He spins around. Huck hoists his head

46

off the bedroll, pricks his ears. A timid growl escapes. They listen. Crackling campfire, creek, and crickets all serenade a symphony accompanied by a west wind that kicks an essence of warm cedar through the damp meadow.

Joe swats Huck away from his bedroll, sits, and pulls his boots off. "I love you, Huck, but you best get used to playing second fiddle. I'm gonna be a daddy. You believe that?" Joe sinks into his bedroll, and Huck curls in next to him. Joe rubs the dog's soft ear. "There's gonna be a boy calling me Dad." He pulls the cover under his chin, crosses his arms under his head, and closes his eyes with a tearful grin. "Man, oh man, I already love him, and he ain't even here yet." The luxury of private weeping. "Thank you, Lord."

Stars sprout and earth rotates as night grows. The Milky Way spills across wide-open space, and below it all, Huck sleeps in a ball next to a few glowing coals as Joe snores. A silhouette emerges—approaches from behind the wall of white-barked aspens. Closing in on Joe. Tall. A cowboy hat cloaks a face. Huck's growl wakes Joe. Instinctively, he sits up from a deep sleep, but before he can remember where the hell he is, a rock cracks the back of his skull. Huck barks incessantly but isn't brave. With a feeble effort to turn toward his attacker, Joe collapses onto his side. Onto the crisp carpet of pine needles. Thought and movement paralyzed by his seizing brain. A pathetic moan encourages the killer to raise the granite rock with both hands and pop the cranium with a final blow to the right temple. Thin skin splits and craters with bone. Blood dribbles, then pools, as gloved hands slide Joe's bedroll away from him. An eye escapes its socket and comes to rest on the bridge of Joe's nose. His hazel iris dilates with death.

In the dead of night, crickets go silent. Joe's colt snorts and tugs against the burlap hobbles tied around his front legs while the killer buckles down the saddlebags. Like a secret witness, Huck watches from a safe distance. Joe lies on his side as if watching the killer roll the bedroll and tie it to the back of the saddle.

A gloved hand works a cold bit into the horse's mouth. The frightened animal's hind legs jig and trample Joe before the killer can get the horse under control and close enough to the corpse. Joe's heavy leg is lifted. His boot shoved through the stirrup—up to the ankle. A serrated pocketknife saws through the burlap hobbles. The instant the horse's legs are free, he twists his head and sidesteps. Joe follows. With a snort, the colt backs, pinning his ears at the body following him. Joe's arms shift above his head as if he has decided to surrender.

"Heeyaw!" the killer screams, and the colt bolts— dragging and bouncing Joe across the meadow as Huck follows them up the ridge and out of sight. Crickets come to life. With both hands, the killer lifts the bloody granite and tosses the evidence into the fire. Cooling ash swarms like scavenging buzzards as Joe's murderer escapes the site of this tragic but accidental death toting the fly rod.

Morning at the ranch is consistent with most preceding mornings. Blue jays squawk. The crippled cat is curled on a stack of firewood on the porch. A frosty dew spreads under the apple orchard as tendrils of smoke climb from the stovepipe, twisting and turning like vines in the atmospheric pressure. The only flaw in this perfect portrait of the West is the green-and-white Calaveras County Sheriff's SUV parked in the driveway.

At the kitchen table, Kate refills Deputy Paul Lipinski's tin cup with coffee while he downs the last of a hearty piece of apple pie. A sticky crumb lingers on a single hair in his red mustache as if one of his many freckles has suddenly slipped out of place. He stands, says, "Thank you," and pats his belly as the radio on his hip squeals. He spins the volume down. "Mr. Rivera is adamant about pressing charges. Please contact me the minute Mr. Quick arrives." He hands Kate his card. "We'll need him to come in and give a statement."

"He need a lawyer?"

"I'm not at liberty to advise you, but I don't think it's necessary at this point. Just have him come in so we can start processing the pieces."

Kate slides the card into her back pocket as she escorts Lipinski to the door. "It'd be extremely helpful if you'd wake Emma Lee. I just need to ask—"

"Nope." Kate shakes her head like an ill-mannered pony. "She was up all night bawlin' and throwin' up. Her and that baby need rest." She opens the front door. "I sure hope Roper didn't do somethin'. He was rantin' like a maniac, said he was gonna kill Joe."

"People make threats all the time, I wouldn't worry." He shakes her hand. "Thanks again for the pie, Ms. Dunnigan."

Kate watches Lipinski pull out of the drive and shuts the door. In no time, she's out the back door and on her way to the Airstream—ignoring the hungry nickers coming from the barn.

The Airstream door is unlocked like always, and Kate sticks her head inside. "Em?" Silence. *Please, just be sleeping.* Kate steps in. Takes four steps through the living room/kitchen/dining room area and wraps her fingers around the bedroom doorknob. "Emma Lee!" She knocks and waits. Takes a deep breath, then twists the knob and opens the door. The double bed is made. Kate glances alongside the bed, checks the shower. Tragedy has cautioned her to expect the worst, but grit forces her to rule it out.

Walking back toward the house, the slight possibility that Em could be sleeping in her old bed in her old room has not been ruled out. Kate hurries. Again, ignoring the hungry horses nickering in the barn.

The doorjamb swells every winter and especially in this wet spring. After two failed attempts to open the door, Kate turns the knob and rams it hard with her shoulder. It gives with a pop. Kate looks around the room that held so much promise. Wallpaper that once was white, now withered and peeling—making the room smell like old books. Em's blue ribbons. Shelves of Breyer horses. Pencil sketches of mountains vistas and riders on the trail. So much of her still here. That familiar motherly panic begins to form—sickening her. She pushes the worry aside. Horses have to be fed.

In the barn, Kate approaches the haystack. Dipping in the front pocket with two bandaged fingers, she pulls a knife and saws at the orange twine on a bale of alfalfa. It pops open like an accordion. Two heavy flakes fall into her arms.

"I already fed." Em lifts the saddle off a black horse tied at the feed manger. Dried sweat coats his short back, leaving a salty white crust.

"Where the hell have you been?" Kate fights to stay calm.

"Went to meet Dad," Em mumbles.

Kate drops the hay. Walks to Em and wants so badly to slap some sense into her child, even beat it into her if it would help. Lost—she struggles to ask. The words will not come. She stares at Em and chews her lower lip. After two deep breaths: "You see him?"

Em turns away and walks the horse to his stall.

Kate follows, asking soft, slow, and steady, "Emma Lee—did—you—see him?"

"I waited there. He said—"

"Where? You waited where?"

Em unbuckles the horse's halter and turns him loose in his stall. He drops and rolls in fresh pine shavings, then jumps up and shakes like a wet dog.

"Em, please tell me where you went?"

"You know."

Kate shakes her head as every nerve in her body fires. "Where?" She has to hear it. Assumptions are too risky.

"Hunt camp." Em's voice cracks as she begins to cry. "I'm sorry, Mom."

"Goddamn it." Kate sits against the feed manger, tasting the shit that just hit the fan.

"He didn't even show up, okay." Em shuts the stall door and sits next to Kate. "I had to. I didn't know what else to do."

Kate wishes Em would laugh, fess up that she's just messing around. One of those bad jokes that you don't realize isn't funny until you tell it out loud. And she's sorry, she won't do it again. Life can go on the way it should. Kate knows too well the suffering to come. How could such a strong woman, built of solid bone, thick skin, nerve, and grit, suddenly want to trade places with that fly feasting on a pile of shit.

Hooves splash and slap through wet gravel as Joe's paint colt trots into the barn. Without his bridle, he tears at the haystack. His saddle hangs sideways. Left stirrup missing. Dried blood crusted on his white legs.

"Oh God." Em rushes over. Runs her hands down the colt's hind legs. "Mom! I can't find where he's bleeding." Looking under his belly for an injury. "There's nothing. No cuts." Em stands and looks at her mom for help. "God, Mom, where's Joe? What if something happened to him?"

"Cowboy justice," Kate whispers as she halters the colt and ties him to the feed manger.

"We gotta find him!"

"I'll call the sheriff—they can send help. If Joe's hurt, there's nothing you can do." Kate holds her hand out, waiting for her little girl to take it. "We pay taxes. Let them bastards do their job." Em's doe eyes look desperate as she takes Kate's hand. "You go get in your old bed and give that baby some rest."

"Mom. I'm so scared."

"I know, sweetie. Don't borrow trouble, we'll worry when we know we got somethin' to worry about. Okay?" She squeezes Em's hand.

"Okay."

"Em . . . you can*not* tell anyone you talked to your father. Understand?"

Em nods and rubs her eyes.

A framed eight-by-ten of happy little Em on Daddy's shoulders. An autographed poster of George Strait grins down from the ceiling as Em falls into her antique bed. Iron springs and Em bounce and groan in unison. Kate pulls Em's boots off just like she has for so many years after a long weekend of junior rodeos. "Want a pair of my sweats?"

"No, I'm fine."

"I'll get your quilt." Kate reaches it off a shelf in the closet and covers Em.

In the fetal position, Em closes her eyes as Kate brushes the hair from her face.

"Get some rest." Kate moves to the faded denim curtains and unties the sashes. The heavy material falls together like hands in prayer and darkens the room. Life looks better in the dark.

"I'll call the sheriff." Kate leaves the door ajar and tries to go quietly, but the creaking wood floor won't allow it. In under a minute, Em is up. Pulling her boots on. Behind the curtain, she unlatches the window and slides it open. The screen pops out as easily as it always has and falls onto the ground.

Kate pulls Deputy Lipinski's card from her back pocket and grabs the phone from the charger. She presses the green call button. The dial tone as intrusive and obnoxious as the thought of Joe cheating on Em with Savannah. Kate hangs up and tosses the card on the counter. "Rotten bastard."

From the junk drawer, Kate brings out a worn address book and flips it open to the letter *C*. Skimming her bandaged fingers down past Joyce Cabett—a best friend through high school last seen or heard from freshman year at San Francisco State. Down past Ike Cagliari, a welder Will never paid for building their pipe roping arena. Stops at Sally Cahill—holds her dirty nail under the name. Sal was the best neighbor a person could have had until she allowed her daughter to babysit two-year-old Em while Kate attended her grandfather's funeral in San Francisco. Sally was the first to accuse Will of inappropriately touching her daughter. No one believed it, including Kate. They never spoke again, and Sal moved to Idaho the next year.

Patrick Callahan's number is there. Faded but there. Kate has always been the kind of woman who is more comfortable doing favors for others, never able to accept them for herself. She needs help and doesn't have single friend left. Patrick is the only option. She dials her brother and waits. His cheerful voice instantly warms her heart as it instructs her to please leave a message and he will call back as soon as he can. *"Don't forget to have a great day."*

"Pat . . . Hi. I wasn't sure this was still your number. Um, it's Kate, remember me? I, uhh . . ." She pauses. Squeezes her brow with her hand. "You said if I ever needed anything to call you." Her voice fighting the lump bloating deep in her throat. "So, I guess . . . that's why I'm callin'." She hangs up quick. Doubts he'll call back, but stares at the phone anyway, willing it to ring.

A cast-iron teakettle simmers on the stove. Through the kitchen window, Kate watches a bay mare nurse her buckskin foal. She can't help but wonder what kind of mother Em could be now with all that has happened.

54

Imagines her grandchild will ride and rope off the well-bred buckskin. How can she protect Em now? Protect her grandchild? Boiling water steams from the kettle, but Kate ignores it, trying to find a way to deal with Em and her father. How did it get to this? An hour passes before Kate realizes she's done nothing but dwell on the past. On Will. This is stupid. Kate occupies her anxiety by scrubbing the refrigerator inside and out.

Carrying a meat loaf sandwich made just the way Em likes it, with pepper jack and barbeque sauce, Kate shuffles down the hall to Em's room. She pushes the door open with her hip and sets lunch on the dresser before noticing she's alone. "Em?" She looks around. "Em?"

Em trots a high-headed sorrel uphill, picking her way through a brushy deer trail—a twenty-minute shortcut to Devil's Nose. Riding bareback, she grabs a fistful of the mare's mane, chokes up on her reins, and kicks the mare into a full-throttle run. The horse struggles to gain elevation, front legs digging, hind legs pushing harder and harder. All Em can think of is Joe. He has to be okay. Dread energizes, forcing her to kick and kick until they top the incline. A few strides farther, then down a gully and up the other side. Her heavy breathing rivals the mare's until they become one rhythmic force. A fire road offers five miles of open track. The mare drops her head and runs as fast as she can. Hooves moving so quick and smooth, it's as if she's flying.

Kate runs into the kitchen, holding Deputy Paul Lipinski's card. Reaches for the phone as it rings and draws back a moment before snagging up the receiver. "Hello?" Hoping she doesn't sound panicked. "Patrick . . . oh, thank God." Her shoulders drop as a shred of relief washes over her. "How soon can you get here?" She waits. Nods. "Okay. I can't talk now, but call me when you get out of the city. I'll explain the whole damn mess." She hangs up. Dials Deputy Lipinski and waits. Biting her thumbnail. "Um, this is Kate Dunnigan. Joe's horse came back without him and had blood all over his legs but not a scratch on him. I think Joe could be hurt and Emma Lee took off lookin' for him, up to Devil's Nose." Kate waits for Lipinski to digest all the information. She agrees when he puts her on hold. She cradles the receiver on her shoulder and takes a glass from the dish drainer. Fills it with cold water from the tap and drinks. *Keep it together.* The glass half empty, she sets it down and takes consecutive long breaths. In deep—through the nose. Out through the mouth until Lipinski is back. "A helicopter?"

A distant whump, whump, whump. A hidden chopper haunts a cloudless sky as Em pushes through another narrow deer trail. Weaving through the shade of thick pines and cedars, her exhausted eyes want to close as they drift along the treetops. A chill shakes her focus back to the forest floor. Crisp pine needles crump and crunch under horse's hooves.

Ahead, the trail widens——pines and cedars thin. A high-pitched yip, then several clear and present yelps, stop Em and her horse in their tracks. Her eyes dart in every direction. Waiting. Listening as movement catches her peripheral vision. Vultures, fwap, fwap, fwap, lifting their heavy wings, exploding from somewhere on her right. Tapping the mare's sides with her spurs, Em reins to the right and guides the horse between boulders. Two coyotes tug at a piece of meat, then examine Em with amber eyes before reluctantly creeping away. Her heart kicking. Her head thumping in her ears as she presses the mare forward. Suddenly, Huck runs out from behind a split juniper, spooking Em and the mare. "Huck!" The dog sucks back for a moment. "Huck, come here, buddy." He darts and disappears into the shadowy forest underbrush. "Huckster!" Em kicks the horse toward the thick manzanita, but the brush is impenetrable. "Shit." The mare spins as Em lifts the reins and rides back to the trail.

Sunlight heats mountain misery, pines, and cedars, causing the forest to smell like a sixty-five-dollar candle. Light spills in sections across the trail and backlights a leg. "Joe!" Em jumps down and runs to it, but stops the minute a boot with a stirrup over it comes into focus. "Joe?" It feels unreal. Her legs are heavy, hard to move, like wading through mud. She wants to leave but wants Joe more. Turn around. Go home. Back to the way things were. Slowly, she steps forward to Joe's mangled and muddy corpse. "Joe!" Rolling him onto his back, she can never unsee the warped skull, the abstract face like a macabre Picasso. A debris-filled socket that once held the hazel eye that could impress her so effortlessly. Shaking, gasping, she steps back, rubs her eyes—wipes them hard. Harder. On her knees, she whispers, "Keep your eyes shut . . . Keep your eyes shut, don't look."

A bald and burly man steps softly out of Em's room, trying to quietly get the door to latch, but he quits after the third attempt. He pulls off heavy black-rimmed glasses with a used syringe in his hand. "I gave her a mild sedative." His gentle voice as caring as his touch against Kate's back as he walks her down the hall.

"Patrick, I told you, she's pregnant."

"It's much less detrimental than the trauma she just experienced."

"Sorry." Kate forces a decent conversation with the brother she hasn't seen in nearly nine years. "I can't believe you retired, thought you loved fixing hearts."

"I retired based on the idea that Bev and I would travel." A sarcastic laugh spurts from somewhere deep inside him. "Listen, you remember Maureen Yamaguchi?"

Kate thinks. "The gal you swore was not your girlfriend?"

"Yes. And for the record, she was more than just a girlfriend. I loved her for a long time. Another story for another time. She was the director of the psychiatric department at Berkeley. She runs a private clinic now. Why don't I call her—see what she suggests?"

"I don't know. There's some things—"

"Kate, she's going to need professional help. You can't expect someone to cope with this type of trauma on their own. If it's the money, please . . . don't worry; I'll take care of it."

"No way. I'm not puttin' this on you."

"Still as stubborn as always. I'm not offering because I feel obligated. I'm insisting because I'm selfish. It'll make me feel good to help." He flops onto a chair at the kitchen table and packs the used syringe into a red plastic box. "You and Em are all I have left. Well, besides Mom. Beverly moved out, somewhat— her things are still there, but I don't think she'll return for them."

"What, when?" Kate slides into the chair at the head of the table, sorry that so much time has passed. Sorry that she allowed her husband to come between them. Sorry that she couldn't tell Patrick she was sorry.

"Four months ago. She went to Paris for a conference and realized she was a lesbian. She is *not* a lesbian."

"You should of called."

"I expected her to realize her error and return. And, I didn't want her angry because I shared her sexual experiments with everyone. Now, I would sincerely enjoy sharing that information with anyone who would care to listen."

"I care." Avoiding holidays, birthdays, Dad's funeral, Patrick's wedding, slowly turned into total dissociation. Giving a shit is for amateurs, but Kate can't help herself. She stands. Walks over to Pat and hugs him long and hard. "I'm sorry."

"Timing is everything. Right now, I need you as much as you need me. And the thought of someone addressing me as 'Uncle Pat' sounds terrific."

"Ought to be somethin' good comes outta this hell, Uncle Pat."

Uncle Pat grins. "I'll call Maureen."

"Be sure and tell her about Bev's lesbianism."

With a hardy laugh, he nods. "She knows."

Clouds churn and swell in a murky morning sky above apple blossoms twitching in the gray drizzle. Steam spouts from a herd of cattle like a candescent fountain. Wetness darkens the log barn and gathers—dripping from the eaves. In their stalls, horses tear at their alfalfa breakfast while Joe's colt waits impatiently for his. Em holds a flake of hay, considers starvation as a form of retaliation against the ignorant beast for killing Joe. "You want this? Huh? You stupid piece of shit." Throwing the hay in his face, Em watches the hungry colt shake tiny dried leaves from his head and eat unoffended.

Like a tombstone, Joe's saddle leans against the feed manger. Em lies on his bedroll and cradles her belly. Crawling under the canvas and wool blankets, Joe's scent is strong—a potpourri of toast, leather, and cow shit. Salty tears saturate her smile as she remembers the first time with Joe under these same blankets—in this very bedroll. How scared she was, but how badly she'd wanted him. As if her body were possessed by an entity that fed off him and never left. That night, Joe had confessed that he loved her and asked if she would please, please, please marry him. She knew she would before he'd asked.

Em looks at her wedding band, the crud and scratches dishonoring it. Flipping the covers aside, she sits up and spits on the ring—polishing it with the tail of her denim shirt. As she holds the ring up to the light, she catches a glimpse of the aluminum fly rod tube back above the tack room door. In an instant, she's up, but time feels misplaced as she works the tube down with a manure rake. Hands shaking and weak, unwilling to cooperate, she unscrews the cap from the tube, like in a dream, where the world is warped and simple tasks become fragmented and damn near impossible. The cap drops in a prolonged moment. Rolls hesitantly across the dirt floor. She tips the case until the three-pieced rod creeps out. Sickening nausea spirals through her.

On the kitchen table, the Calaveras Yellow Pages advertise six cemeteries. Sunset and Murphy's take up an entire page. Kate circles the number for Sunset.

"Mom!" Em explodes through the back door, waking Uncle Pat on the sofa sleeper. "Mom!"

Kate slaps the phone book shut.

"Did you put this away?" Em holds the fly rod out with both hands.

"Why?"

"'Cause Joe took it with him! It wasn't with his stuff when the colt came back. I checked! I specifically checked!" Em's arms bounce. "How'd it get back here?" Her eyes jump around the room. "Who put it back above the tack room?" Out of breath, her heart racing, anxious for a reasonable answer.

The fly rod and tube decorate the kitchen table like a vulgar centerpiece as Deputy Lipinski sits, filling out his report. "Who knew where the fishing pole belongs?"

"Rod." Em crosses her arms and leans against the doorway.

"Rod who?" Lipinski asks as he writes.

"It's a fishing *rod.* A pole goes in the ground." Em smirks. Lipinski looks up without lifting his head.

"What about Roper?" Kate offers. "You need to talk to that boy, he was threatin' Joe, I could hear him all the way over here." Everyone stares at the rod, analyzing the possibility of Roper being a killer.

"I can't picture him doing it." Em cracks her knuckles. "He woulda hired someone, he's got money. And I've never seen him crazy mad like that, and we been best friends since forever."

"Why bother with the rod?" Uncle Pat wonders out loud.

Em suddenly stunned, her mouth drops and she looks like she's just lost her innocence. Her eyes move to Kate as Lipinski observes her.

"What?" Uncle Pat asks.

Kate deflects. "I'm sure this is all just a——"

"My dad," Em says. "He could of . . . He loved that rod. And I told him what Roper said, and . . ."

Kate grins and runs her fingers across her forehead. Down her temple. "I don't think—"

"What's his name?" Lipinski presses his pen on his pad.

"Will—William Dunnigan." Em immediately wishes she hadn't spoken. She pictures her dad, his enormous smile, the way he has always defended her, regardless of right or wrong. He would *never* point a finger at her, never suggest her as a murder suspect. The air turns thick, and breathing becomes a task. "I need to find Huck." Em scrambles out the door.

"Who's Huck? I have to complete her statement." Lipinski looks back and forth between Kate and Uncle Pat.

"Huck's Joe's dog, and you're wastin' your time anyway. Her dad ain't been around for . . . gosh"—Kate shrugs—"gotta be fifteen, sixteen years."

"Perhaps he contacted her. It is possible. Or, Em could have found him. Google, Facebook, there are multiple ways." Uncle Pat's authoritative conclusion forces Kate's unease to surface.

"He was a *rotten, no-good son of a bitch* and would *never* come back. Last I heard, he was on the run for sellin' fake Navajo rugs, went to Brazil or somethin'. Maybe even back to Australia."

"Why would your daughter consider him a suspect?" Lipinski asks.

"Goddamn! She's pregnant, her husband's accused of raping a girl—now he's dead. She finds him all tore up and her baby ain't got a father. There's a real good chance she ain't thinkin' clearly." Kate finally takes a breath. Lipinski pets his mustache and looks to Uncle Pat.

"Em may be so desperate to make sense of current events that she's focusing on finding empathy for Joe by crafting him into the victim role. And the fact that she must carry a deep-rooted resentment for her father's abandonment. I think Kate has a valid point." Patrick offers.

Lipinski slaps his notebook closed. "We don't have enough evidence to support further investigation. Mr. Quick's death appears to be accidental, and therefore the charges that were filed against him will be dismissed."

"An autopsy could reveal evidence, right?" Uncle Pat asks.

"That's the coroner's decision." Lipinski grasps the doorknob.

"I believe family has the right to request one. Unless Calaveras County has jurisdiction over California law."

63

Uncle Pat seems to know his rights. "Especially if we pay for it."

Kate slams her palms on the table. "That poor boy has no family but us—let him rest in peace!"

Hugging her knees, Em sits on Joe's bedroll in the barn. Her cell phone ready and waiting in her hand. Ready and waiting to reveal Dad's guilt or innocence. Either will surely devastate their rekindled relationship.

"Hi, sweetie." Kate sits next to her. "How you doin'?"

"This is crazy, right?"

"We passed crazy days ago." Kate wraps an arm around Em and squeezes.

"If I call Dad and accuse him, he'll take off again, I'll never see him."

"I wish you wouldn't worry about your dad. He ain't comin' back and you know that."

"Why would you say that?"

Kate stares at Em like she's a stranger. Improv, insults, and a pocketknife were tools Kate kept ready at all times. "Let's talk to Roper. See how he acts."

Em buries her head between her knees and offers Kate her cell. "Call him."

"No way. I want to look him in the eye. I've known that boy since he was five, and I'll know if he's been up to no good."

"There's a roping in Moke Hill tonight. He'll be there."

"How about you go take a nice, warm bath. That always makes you feel better."

Em hugs her mom and kisses her cheek.

"Uncle Pat has a friend he wants you to talk to. She's a big-time expert, comin' all the way from the Bay Area to help you out. Should be here around three. Maybe I can talk to her when you're done." Kate's crossed eyes and silly smile force a grin out of Em.

From the kitchen window, Kate watches Em and Maureen walk the path through the orchard and disappear behind the oaks at the pond. The urge to know what Em is sharing forces Kate to concoct reasons to walk down—certain to listen as long as possible before interrupting. *Take them cookies? Too obvious. Ask Maureen to stay for dinner? No. Stop*, Kate thinks. *Leave them alone. Give Em the chance to heal.*

"Trauma is an emotional response to a terrible event such as an accident, a violent act, physically abuse, sexual assault, or even a natural disaster. Immediately following the event, a person is likely to experience shock and, very likely, denial." Maureen Yamaguchi and Em sit on a log overlooking the pond. "It's the mind's way of protecting us."

"You think I'm crazy?" Em reaches down and plucks a red flower.

"Not at all, but I do believe professional help is necessary. Would you be willing to commit to treatment?"

"Couldn't hurt, I guess." Em hands Maureen the flower. "Indian paintbrush."

"Beautiful. Did Native Americans paint with these?"

"They used them to poison their enemies." Em turns. "Mom?"

"Hi. Sorry to interrupt. I'm starting dinner—can you stay, Maureen?" Kate sets her palms on her lower back and rocks onto her heels.

"No, thank you for asking. I have to get back to the clinic."

"How 'bout a steak to-go plate? Homemade potato salad."

"I'm a vegetarian, but I do appreciate the thought. I'll speak to Pat and be on my way." Maureen stands, daintily pinching the Indian paintbrush between her thumb and index finger.

As sunlight fades, floodlights pop on in the Mokelumne Hill Arena. Dozens of riders lope in the same direction to warm up their horses—swinging ropes in a cloud of dust. "Get signed up, guys! We're starting in ten minutes," a woman's voice announces over a loudspeaker. Savannah Rivera rides a beefy red roan past Em.

"Hey, Savannah." Em lets the plastic door on the blue outhouse slam behind her.

"Oh, hey, Em, didn't see you." Savannah sips from a strawberry-kiwi wine cooler. "I'm super sorry about Joe."

Em studies Savannah and crosses her arms. "Why you sorry?"

Savannah rolls her eyes and raises her brow. "Ughhh, 'cause—it's, like, super sad?"

"Why the hell would you be sad? Or sorry, after what he did to you?"

"Forget it." Savannah rides away sucking down a wine cooler.

"You're sorry 'cause you're lying, huh? I know you! You're a lying little bitch!"

Roper trots by. "Knock it off, Em."

"She's lying, Rope. Supposed to be pregnant and she's drinking? Give me a break."

"Let's go." Kate walks up and snatches Em's arm. "I talked to him. He didn't do anything. It was just an accident, okay?"

"But, Mom, Savannah's lying!"

"Doesn't matter—it's over. Understand? Done." Kate puts her arm around Em and walks her away.

"This is not right, Mom. I mean, does she even realize?"

"Em! Listen here, damn it." Kate steps in front of her daughter. "Look at me." Em crosses her arms, still pissed, but eventually obeys. "I want you to understand something—believing a thing *never* makes it true."

At 3:20 a.m., clouds cover the bottom of a waning half-moon. Mr. and Mrs. Rivera sleep in their California king bed, in their upstairs master suite, in their five-thousand-square-foot custom Colonial. Fuck them and the well-bred, overpriced, ill-broke horses they rode in on.

A shadow spills down the mahogany staircase, along the family-photo-lined hall. A lanky cowboy silhouette approaches a picture of twelve-year-old Roper with braces atop a white horse. The shadow stops in front of an airbrushed portrait of Mr. and Mrs. Rivera, then moves silently past a snapshot of seven-year-old Roper holding his baby sister Savannah's hand. Past Roper's high school graduation. Slowly darkening a recent shot of Roper and Savannah frolicking in the Maui surf,

Savannah's bikini top unable to keep up with the surf and her blossoming bosom. The hall dead-ends at a white door. A gloved hand reaches out. Twists the brass knob.

Above a purple comforter, Savannah sleeps on her side like an unholy cherub. Her plump lips spread, exposing an overbite suitable for breathing. Flaunting a leg designed for Broadway. Worn black boots shuffle across thick pink carpet as gloved fingers tighten their grip on a jagged hunk of granite. The moment Savannah is within reach, the killer lifts the rock and whips it down. Up and down and up and down again. Smack, smack, smack, pounding the girl's brunette head. She doesn't move, doesn't make a sound, doesn't seem to mind being killed. A long, satisfying breath accompanies an appreciative moment. Then the second series of smacks. Deep into the girl's abdomen. The killer's cowboy hat rears and bucks with each strike. Then, like a caring mother, the gloved hand drags the purple comforter over the girl and tucks her in. A bloody glove brushes bloody hair from her bloody face. The killer slams the door on the way out.

Kate slams a cast-iron skillet onto the stove as Uncle Pat drifts in with hints of Old Spice trailing him.

"Jeez, you smell like Dad." Kate layers the skillet with thick bacon.

"You act like him." He smirks, pouring coffee into a red tin cup. Bacon sizzles and pops in the pan. "She's going to be fine."

Kate shakes her head. "What'd Maureen think after talkin' to her?"

"She can't disclose information to me or anyone else."

"Thought you two are close?"

"We are, but patient privileges don't allow her to share information. She could lose her license."

"She can't tell you anything? At all?"

"Katie, it's complicated."

"No shit." She shoots Uncle Pat a look meant to remind him that she's not an uneducated bumpkin.

After long sips of coffee followed by an uncomfortable silence, Uncle Pat breaks. "She said that Em has been traumatized and that most patients suppress memories when something that drastic happens. It's the mind's way of defending itself during extremely difficult situations. She suspects that, in time, Em will accept the reality of what happened and relinquish her blame and/or guilt. We agree that weekly visits are essential to recovery."

"You're a doctor. You have that same patient privilege thing?" Kate flips the dripping bacon with a fork. "Do you?" Kate looks at him.

"I would *never* share information about my patients. It would be unethical. Why?"

Hot grease pops onto Kate's hand as she unnecessarily flips the bacon—eyes watering. "Are you crying?" he asks.

"It's this goddamn smoke."

"Katie, we don't need doctor-patient privileges. I'm always on your side. No matter what." Uncle Pat rubs her shoulder. "It's okay to cry; being tough all the time isn't a virtue."

"Remember when Will left?" Her faded brown eyes beg for help.

"Yes."

"He was always up to no good, you know. I showed up one night, up at his hunting camp."

Two Calaveras County Sheriff's vehicles roll down the driveway and stop at the house.

"Good Lord, now what?" Kate stomps outside as Officer Hernandez and Officer Ladd follow Lipinski to the porch.

"Hello, Ms. Dunnigan. Is Emma Lee home?" Lipinski asks.

"She's sleeping. Why?"

"Savannah Rivera was attacked early this morning."

"Attacked? What do you mean, attacked?"

"That's privileged information at this point. A detective would like to ask Emma Lee a few questions. I have to bring her in."

"But she's been right here all night, and she would never—"

"Could you get her please, ma'am?"

"Is Savannah okay?"

"I can't share that information."

"Holy hell." Kate's heart begins to flap in her chest, like a bird trying to escape an awful fate. She staggers to the screen door and grips the handle but can't bring herself to open it as smoke from burning bacon goes unnoticed.

Lipinski drives away followed by a sedan with Emma Lee in the back seat. Watching from the front porch, Kate turns to Uncle Pat. "When's it gonna stop?" That familiar sick feeling of helplessness boils up inside her. The feeling she thought she had learned to conquer years ago. A woodpecker knocks hard against the eaves on the side of the house, like an intrusive jackhammer. Kate hurls a piece of firewood at him. The bird squawks and flies into a nearby tree. "Sons a bitches . . . always somethin'. *Always*."

"Kate, is Will capable of this?"

"Of course." Kate's voice thickening. "If he was still alive."

A heavy steel door shuts with a clang. In the tight questioning room, mint-colored cinder blocks radiate a frothy green hue, accentuating Detective Ed Rocha's alien-like features. Round, dark eyes. A compact, thin-lipped mouth below a flat nose. An abnormally large bald head carried around on a delicate neck and diminutive body. The windowless room narrowly accommodates a small table and three metal folding chairs. With his elbows on the table, Rocha steeples his fingers under his chin. "We have witnesses that claim you were harassing Savannah at a roping competition last night." His voice surprisingly deep and smelling of coffee and cigarettes. He slides Em an eight-by-ten close-up of Savannah's mutilated face. Em glances at the evidence that resembles roadkill. Meat and muscle, flesh and hair, tendons and tissue.

"Doesn't look like her." She pushes the photo away, closes her eyes, and lifts her brow. Squeezing unrecognizable Savanah out of her mind. Rocha studies Em as she rubs her eyes with her sleeves. "Keep your eyes shut, don't look. I have to go to the bathroom." She says, then stands, clinging to the edge of the table with both hands.

"You just went." Rocha pushes the picture back to her. It's too much, and she can't stop it—she covers her mouth, but the vomit escapes.

"Don't look," She utters and wobbles. Her chin catches the edge of the table just before she hits the floor.

"They took her to Mark Twain Hospital." Kate closes her beat-up flip phone and inhales that new-car smell of Uncle Pat's BMW before locating the button to roll the window down. Thick grass carpets her foothills as they wind down the two-lane bordering the ranch. "Should have plenty a feed this year."

"Christ, after what you just told me, I'd say that's the least of your worries." Uncle Pat fists the steering wheel, then attempts to pass a hay truck. "Fuck! You should know, I feel very uncomfortable with this." Head-on, a black Cadillac forces him back behind the hay truck. "Tell her the truth. You asked for my help, and I think the hospital is the perfect opportunity." He passes and veers in front of the hay truck. Looks into his side mirror and accepts the driver's middle finger waving out the window.

I know that guy, Kate is about to say as she squints and looks out the rear window, but an army-green peacoat in the back seat distracts her. "Is that Dad's old wool coat?"

"Yes. You can't buy them anymore."

Something passes through Kate before she realizes it's a twinge of happiness at the thought of Patrick wearing Dad's old coat. Glad at the possibility he wasn't as injured by Dad's heartless management.

72

They ride five miles before Patrick speaks. "If you doubt my authority, consider Freud. He believed that lancing old wounds and dealing with that pain is the only way to transcend our past and overcome our neuroses. That's *exactly* what this is."

A poster of a fully formed fetus sucking its thumb, a red plastic needle disposal box, and a corner chair piled with Em's clothes decorate the hospital room. White tape covers the stitches in Em's chin, and an IV pumps fluid into her vein as she stares at the poster. Lysol and fresh ivory enamel infuse the cold room as the door opens and Kate peeks in. "Hi, hon."

"Mom. Hi, Uncle Pat." Em's voice is throaty and tired.

Kate hugs her. "How ya feelin'?"

"Hungry, actually."

"Good. That's a good sign. What did the doctor say?" Uncle Pat inspects her stitches.

"They're running tests. They took a bunch a blood, and now my arm really, really hurts. So does my head. And my chin is numb." She smacks her chin with the back of her fingers.

"I'm going to get you a sandwich and speak to your doctor, alright?" Uncle Pat eyes Kate.

"Okay. Thanks, Uncle Pat." Em smiles. As Uncle Pat goes, he shoots Kate one last insistent glare.

"Aw, sweetie." Kate rubs Em's arm. "I love you so much."

"Love you too, Mom."

"Listen, I have to know something. It's important, okay?"

Em waits.

73

Kate takes a deep breath. "You said you talked to your dad. That he was gonna meet you?"

"Yeah?"

Not the answer Kate wants. Not even close. She takes Em's hands and squeezes them. *Best not to consider this any longer. Do it!* "Your dad is dead." Ripped off like a full-body Band-Aid. "There ain't no way you talked to him."

"Not funny, Mom."

"No, it's not. Now, no more bullshit. He's dead and you know it 'cause you were there."

Em pulls her hands away and takes time to consider the possibilities. "I just talked to him." She drops her legs off the bed. "What are you doing?"

"Trying to help you get a grip on reality." That was harsh. Probably too much.

"Trying keep us apart? You jealous? Is that it?" Em wipes her eye.

"I'm just trying to help. I'm sorry to have to make you remember, but—"

"You're seriously fucked up. You're the one needs a psychiatrist!" Em rubs both eyes.

"Em, come on now. You were there when it happened."

"When what happened?"

"I killed him. And buried him. You just don't want to remember . . . hunting camp." Kate watches Em's conclusion build.

"I thought it was Dad. I thought maybe he was doin' this—but I totally get it now." Panic. Buzzing. Em swats at her left ear and squints, then drags her fingers across her eyes.

"Please don't rub your eyes. You know what happened, don't let him ruin you."

"You're a bitter old bitch who's terrified of being alone." Em yanks her IV out, and blood splatters the linoleum. "You lost Dad, and I'm all that's left."

"Em, stop! Get back in bed."

Em opens and shuts her eyes. The room is hazy and obscure, like looking underwater. "Do you have my phone? You take it?" She searches her clothes piled on the chair.

"I'm gonna get Uncle Pat." Kate rushes out.

Em finds her phone, then pulls her jeans on under her gown. "Keep your eyes shut. Don't look," she whispers twice as she wiggles the sweatshirt on over the gown, then slips on UGGs. While feeling her way out of the room, she dials Dad.

Through swinging *Staff Only* double doors, Em stumbles down the corridor. "Dad? Thank God, Mom's at it again. Sayin' you're dead!" Em pulls open the stairwell door and exits. "I know, that's exactly what I said." Her voice and steps echo all four floors. "She killed Joe and did her best to kill little Savannah. She thinks she's protecting me, and she'd do *anything* to keep that stupid ranch." Em sits on a cold aluminum step. "Yeah . . . okay, I call him right now. I'll meet you there tomorrow . . . I'm sorry too. I love you." She hangs up and digs Rocha's card from her sweatshirt.

In his office, Detective Rocha sits behind cigarette smoke and a chaotic desk bound on both sides by gray metal filing cabinets. The soft buzz of an air filter struggles to keep up while Rocha tokes under a *No*

Smoking sign. With the phone pinched between his ear and shoulder, he writes on a pink pad in capital letters—*KATHERINE DUNNIGAN.* "Uh-huh, age?" He writes *51.* "Approximate height and weight?" *5'4''. 130 lbs. Mark Twain Hospital.* "You need to come in, Emma Lee, finish your statement." Rocha tears the note from the pad. "Hello? Hello?"

"Hello. Can I help you?" A uniformed dispatcher requiring little effort to impersonate Mrs. Potato Head plants herself in a snug Naugahyde chair and smiles at Uncle Pat. It screeches under the load as she swaps her Diet Dr Pepper for a bag of microwave popcorn. The front office of the Calaveras County Sheriff's Department represents the 1970s inferior design. A faded ficus tree clings to dark wood paneling as Uncle Pat brushes past.

"I'm Kate Dunnigan. I need to talk to someone about the attacks on Savannah Rivera and Joe Quick. I think my daughter might have—"

Rocha slaps the pink note on the dispatcher's desk and walks away. "I called Lipinski, he's at the hospital locating the daughter. I want an APB on the mother."

"Ed?" The dispatcher says with sweet sarcasm.

"*What?*" Rocha's annoyance is blatant.

"This lady would like to speak with you about Savannah Rivera."

Rocha turns back.

The dispatcher reads the note, looks at Kate, then back at the note. She balls up the pink piece of paper and tosses it at Rocha. "This *is* Kate Dunnigan, *Detective.*"

He inspects Kate and offers a routine smile to the dispatcher. "Wonderful. Follow me, Ms. Dunnigan." At the end of the corridor, Rocha points an upturned palm above a set of orange plastic chairs. "Have a seat, I'll be right with you." Kate and Uncle Pat obey as Rocha steps into his office. A consistent and hushed pounding escapes from behind the steel lockup door. A small one-way window rattles with each bang. Someone wants out. Staring at the scuffed parquet, Kate chews her lower lip, unable to come up with a better option.

"There is no other way to go about this, Kate," Uncle Pat reassures her and sets his hand on her shoulder. "You're doing the right thing."

Lipinski escorts Em in through a back door, her hands cuffed in front of her. Kate rushes over and cradles Em's face in her hands. "Are you okay?"

Without hesitation, Em shoves Kate into the opposite wall. "Why isn't she cuffed? She's slaughtering people, and you frigin' idiots are *arresting me*?" Nothing makes sense. She wants Joe. Wants to go home, but like in a bad dream, for some crazy reason, it's impossible.

"We're just holding you," Rocha explains, emerging from his office. The banging coming from behind the cell door stops as Lipinski unlocks it. "Get back and sit down *now*, Ramona."

"Can I braid your hair, pleeeeeease?" Ramona begs as Lipinski forces Em through the door.

"Hands to yourself, Ramona," Lipinski warns before slamming the door.

The jingle of keys locking the steel dead bolt punch Kate in the gut. Years of turbulence release like a cloud burst. Light-headed, she bends over, bracing her hands against her knees. "Let her go." She takes inhales and stands upright. "Let her go. She's right, I did it! I killed Joe. And that nasty little bitch too." Kate grabs Uncle Pat, presses up close, and whispers, "Get her outta here, she can't take this, not with that baby. You promised. *You* promised." Rocha gathers Kate's wrists behind her and sets a cuff. "I'll tell ya everything." Kate spins around and faces Rocha, offering her both hands for cuffing. "Full confession. But first, you let her go home. She's exhausted. You got me, you don't need her. She's innocent. It's me, that's what I came to tell you." It comes out so easy that Kate momentarily convinces herself.

Uncle Pat removes his glasses and scrubs his brow. Rocha crosses his arms and widens his stance as Lipinski watches and waits.

"A mother's and child's health is in your hands, Detective. I cannot conceive of an unsympathetic jury if something were to go wrong."

Kate leans into Rocha's face, eye to eye, tears streaming. "I ain't sayin' a word 'til you release her."

From behind the cell door, the pounding begins again. "Get her out of here," Rocha orders.

Kate closes her eyes as Rocha cuffs her.

"Thank you, Maureen. Your help is immeasurable. I don't know what she's capable of." A dying cell phone beeps as Uncle Pat struggles to find the outlet in Kate's dark kitchen. "I can have her to your facility Monday morning if you have a room available?" After listening to Maureen explain ideal treatment, Uncle Pat shakes his head. "What if she doesn't want to go? I can't force her." He smooths what's left of his hair.

In the questioning room, Kate looks up at a blinking red light on the camera peering down at her from the corner. Rocha licks his front teeth, back and forth, and waits for more. "When I overheard Roper tell Em what Joe had done to Savannah, I just snapped. I couldn't sit back and watch my daughter suffer through a trial. She'd *have* to side with him no matter what, and that would mean a lawyer, and a lawyer means money they didn't have. Then I'd have to put up the ranch to defend him. And there ain't no way, come hell or high water, I'm losin' the ranch." *What a cliché*, Kate thinks and crosses her arms. "What do you really need to know?"

"Why Savannah?"

"Finish cleanin' up the mess Joe left. Em didn't need any more triggers."

"Triggers?"

"That's the wrong word. You know, *reminders* . . . is what I meant. I'm really tired, gotta be after midnight. I'm done."

Spread out across the sofa sleeper, Uncle Pat snores until a bang against the screen door jolts him awake. Staring into blackness, he sits up. Waits. Listens. The hum of the refrigerator and the soft bong of wind chimes lull him back to sleep. In no time, there it is again—a clear and present bang against the screen door, causing him to shoot up.

From the window, he can see the top half of the door under the porch light. No one is there. The porch creaks. He stumbles over his shoes, then feels for his glasses on the coffee table but only finds his cell phone. The glow from the cell enables him to locate his glasses and put them on. With a shaking finger, he dials *9*, then *1*, and waits. Another bang forces him back to the window. Peeking through the side of the curtain. Nothing. "Who is it?" Nothing. "Okay, well, I called the police!" His voice cracks as he grabs the heavy poker leaning near the woodstove. "They'll be here any minute." Two bangs cause him to raise and ready the poker. "Who's there, *damn it*?" He looks out the window. Bang. The screen door bounces twice. Trembling, Uncle Pat swings open the front door to find Huck wagging his tail. "Oh, good God." He leans the poker next to the door and pats his thumping chest as he opens the screen for Huck. "You practically gave me a heart attack, mister."

Early the next morning, Huck follows Uncle Pat and a plate of fried eggs, with bacon and toast, down the hall to Em's room. "You already had yours," he whispers to Huck as he knocks on Em's door.

Huck barges in and curls up next to Em as she wakes. "Huck!" She hugs and kisses and rubs his ears as he moans with pleasure. "Hi, buddy."

"He arrived late last night."

"Oh my gosh, Huckleberry, I missed you. Where have you been—huh?" She sits up.

"I made breakfast." He hands her the plate.

"Thanks." She stabs the yokes with her fork, and they bleed under the bacon and onto the buttered toast. "Mmm, I don't know . . . I feel kinda queasy." Em hands the plate back to him.

"Maybe later, then." Uncle Pat opens the curtains, allowing the rising sun to light the room. "I'll make you a cup of tea. And crackers. That should help with nausea."

Em snuggles with Huck. "You don't have to take care a me, Uncle Pat, I'm a big girl."

"I know, but I want to, so . . . Look, I'd like you to come home with me. Maureen has offered to let you stay at her clinic for a few days or whatever you, uh, it's in Half Moon Bay. You can rest and focus on yourself. They have beautiful rooms overlooking the ocean. Wonderful food. It'll be kind of like a vacation. And, when you're ready . . . you can stay with me, or you can have the pool house, whichever you like."

"Sounds great." Em nods.

"Really?"

"Yeah. Soon as I see Dad, we'll go. He's waiting for me up at camp."

"Call him. Have him come here."

"I would, but he's already up there—no cell service."

"I'd love to see your father, mind if I tag along?"

Em hesitates. "I don't wanna talk about Mom, at all. Okay?"

"Fair enough. I'll pack some food." Halfway out the door, he stops. "Em, I hope you can comprehend . . . I, uh. I want you to know I love you and I'm going to do everything possible to help. Okay?"

"Okay." She doesn't doubt him and smiles. The anticipation of seeing Dad sort of soothes the pain of losing Joe. "I'll saddle a horse for you. Do you even know how to ride?"

"Not at all."

"I'll get you a hat and some boots. Pretty sure Mom still has some of Dad's stuff hidden in her closet."

Clutching his cell to his ear, Uncle Pat paces the front porch and struggles to keeps his panicked voice to a whisper. "She agreed to go to the clinic but wants to see her father first." The wind chimes bang and bong, and Uncle Pat stops them with his hand. "She talks to him on the damn phone—thinks he is going to meet her up there, and I agreed to go. What the hell could I do?" Grasping the porch post, he takes a seat on the steps. "Oh, I can certainly prove it to her."

Maureen's voice comes through the phone, loud and clear. "*How?*"

"I am not at liberty to say . . . but if I were able to show her something that may trigger her memory? Should I?"

"Absolutely!"

A black cowboy hat tilts on Uncle Pat's head as he grips the saddle horn and follows Em. Blackberry bushes coat the sides of the shaded trail, forcing Em to pluck a few and pop them in her mouth as they ride by. "Like blackberries?" Em asks.

"No, I don't care for the seeds, they stick in my teeth." Uncle Pat stops his horse and climbs off, groaning. "Ohhhhh, my everything hurts. I may walk for a while." He digs the heels of his black boots into the red clay, then stretches his fingers in the direction of his toes.

With another handful of berries in her mouth, Em twists back toward Uncle Pat. "We'll be there in twenty minutes. Dad'll have a fire and hopefully a skillet of trout. He always starts cooking as soon as the sun gets two fingers above Squaw Ridge. We'd eat and watch the sunset." Em laughs. "He'd give me a cup of blackberry juice and—" She stops and stares at the purple stains on her fingers. A queasy feeling takes hold of her. Her mouth begins to water, and for some reason, she suddenly wants to cry.

"He was a good dad, huh?" Uncle Pat stretches his arms above his head.

"Yeah." Em spits the blackberries from her mouth.

"Why would he leave you for all those years?"

"Ask him." Em rides away.

Veronica Ames—public defender—Calaveras County. A fidgety young woman who seems to go to great lengths to avoid eye contact. Currently obsessed with picking lint balls off her white sweater. "I'm asking you to help me help you. Okay, Ms. Duncan?" She waits a long, uncomfortable while for an answer.

"Dunnigan. Not Duncan. And, I don't need a lawyer." *Especially one that can't even get my fucking name right.* Uncomfortable in her extra-large jumpsuit, Kate nervously pushes her sweaty palms down her orange jumpsuit thighs.

"Are you officially refusing legal counsel? You understand I'm a public defender. You don't have to pay me."

"Get what you pay for," Kate mumbles.

"Excuse me?"

"I did it. End of story. I don't want to go to trial." *I'm not going to trial. No way.*

"It's my responsibility to make sure you're aware of the consequences, regardless of how you plea, you have rights. And there is a possibility of sanity issues."

Hunting camp is perched on a parcel of meadow between Squaw Ridge and Lost Lake. A deep, dark hidden lake that surfaces at timberline. In the meadow, one massive juniper reaches out across a log-lined camp. Its roots like gnarled fingers, desperately searching for something.

"Wow, this is beautiful." Uncle Pat dismounts.

Em trots past the juniper and toward the lake. "Dad!

Uncle Pat unstraps his dad's wool peacoat from behind his saddle and puts it on, exposing a folding shovel as Em rides back.

"He's not here." Concern smothers Em. "God, what the heck. He said he'd be here." She checks her phone for a signal, lifting it in every direction.

The sun sinks below Squaw Ridge, sending a wave of deep violet into an ocean of orange and blue. "I'm almost sixty, and this is the finest sunset I have ever seen," Uncle Pat confesses through the last bite of a chunky-peanut-butter-and-jelly sandwich. "I can see why your father loved this place."

Em zips her coat and stacks rocks into a fire ring. *Dad hasn't even been here.* "Where is he? Something's wrong."

With shovel in hand, Uncle Pat walks stiff-legged to the giant juniper, stopping at the large triangular rock under it, and kneels.

Em watches him struggle to roll the saddle-size hunk of granite. With a mighty groan, he lifts and flips it. "What are you doing?"

"Trying to figure out why your mother would lie to you."

84

"Because she's insane, and she could never deal with Dad dumping her. Made me and that bullshit ranch her life."

"Well, she insisted that if I didn't believe her story about your father, that I should dig under this rock." He stabs the shovel into the fresh dirt. Outlining the removed rock.

"You think she's full of it too, don't ya?" Em scoops pine needles and sets them in the rock fire ring.

"She does have a morbid obsession with that ranch and an idealistic lifestyle." He digs.

"I used to feel sorry for her. So did everyone else, and she *loved* it. Anytime anyone was around, all she'd talk about is how Dad left her and how heartbroken and miserable she was. Just became a pathetic victim after a while. It's why she doesn't have any friends." Em tosses pine cones into the ring. "What'd she say's under there?"

"The truth."

Em gathers twigs. "You're being weird."

"I know, but I have to do this. Maureen thinks I should show you the truth. It's somewhat like rebooting your memory." He shovels harder and faster.

"What truth?" Em places twigs on pine cones.

"Can you remember the last time you were here? With your father?" Sweat rolls from under the black hat.

Staring into the purple sunset, Em recalls Dad. He's kneeling over a cast-iron skillet of sizzling trout and scraping the browning skins with a spatula. Dad letting her reel in those fish with his fly rod. The way the rod jumped and pulled in her hands. "*Keep the tip up,*" he'd constantly remind her. Swimming in the lake, because

85

they had caught their limit by noon. Picking wildflowers to bring back to Mom. Filling the old coffee can with blackberries. "Yeah, I remember. I remember everything."

"Do you remember your mother arriving that evening?"

"She never came up here. It was *always* only me and Dad." Em tosses wood into the fire ring.

"Your mom said she rode up here to surprise you." Uncle Pat digs efficiently for a man who has probably never handled a shovel.

Resisting the urge to argue, Em strikes a wooden match and watches it burn out. Squinting, she kneels and lights another. The flame burns her fingers, and she drops the match onto the pine needles.

"You know what else she told me?"

"I don't care! You promised you wouldn't talk about her!" Leaning back on her knees, Em watches a tiny flame develop, then struggle to live.

Digging in rhythmic tempo, Uncle Pat raises his voice with unusual firmness. "She said he had gotten you drunk. He gave you blackberry juice mixed with sloe gin." Dirt piling and rising under the juniper like a polluted tide.

"Stop it. Just stop!" Em stares into the flames licking skyward and rubs her eyes. Flaming explosions jolt her brain, and a vivid picture of her father handing her a red tin cup flashes like lightning. She squeezes her eyes shut tight and wipes hard, then opens them wide, trying to see through the blur. Swaying, she goes from her knees to sitting with legs stretched in front of her.

Uncle Pat slams the shovel into the dirt again and again, but Em fixates through the foggy haze on Uncle

Pat's hat—moving back and forth and back and forth. Suddenly, the storm in her head subsides and the fragmented visions come into focus. Her young voice whispers, *"He gave me blackberry juice."* Em lies back, pressing her palms deep into her eyes, then sees and hears the girl as if she were right there next to her.

"Dad filled the cup with blackberry juice from his jar, 'member? Sittin' by the fire, and it looked like the flames were in his jar when he drank, and I laughed. 'Member? I laughed so hard that I had to go to the bathroom. Dad followed me to that big juniper tree, and I told him I could do it myself. Said I was twelve and didn't need no help. But then, when I got all done— I couldn't stand up—got real dizzy and fell over. 'Member? Then . . . I kinda sorta woke up and Dad was on top a me. His hat was moving—up and down, and up and down, and I couldn't move, and I couldn't breathe. His face looked funny at first like he was tryin' to make me laugh. But then the stabbing hurt inside made me cry. I wanted to cry loud but couldn't 'cause he was squishing me. Then . . . the noise. 'Member? The loud CRACK noise? Like when Dad spilt firewood. Then he was squishing me even more. Then a worse CRACKING noise, and Mom was there! She had a rock in her hands, and she looked crazy and really, really mad. She held the rock up, way up, over her head, and she smashed it into Dad's head. She hit him again and blood got in my eyes. Lots and lots a blood got in my eyes. 'Member? It felt weird . . . sticky, and all warm, and I couldn't see nothin'. Mom grabbed my arm and jerked me up, and dragged me outta there. Away from Dad. And she was yelling, "KEEP YOUR EYES SHUT! DON'T LOOK!"

"Keep your eyes shut! Don't look." Em wipes her eyes and stands.

"Em, you have to see this, you have to understand what happened. Your mother was trying to protect you." The sound of the shovel piercing the earth turns to the sound of rock cracking skull—again and again, as Uncle Pat hits something solid. He drops to his knees and digs with his hands. "Look! Jesus Christ, she wasn't lying, Em. Your dad *is* dead." He leans into the grave and lifts a dirty skull. "I'm so sorry, Em, but you have to see the tru—"

"Don't look!" Em slams a rock into the side of Uncle Pat's head, and the black Stetson flies across the grave as he collapses. His broken glasses fall alongside Will's warped skull. CRACK! Blood splatters the dirty skull and glasses.

Leaning against the wall in the questioning room, Kate's orange jumpsuit clashes with the minty-green cinder blocks. The door buzzes, and Miss Ames comes in with an armful of files. "Sorry to keep you waiting. I just received a phone call. Please, sit down." Kate straightens as Miss Ames takes a seat on the cold metal chair. "The good news is that Savannah Rivera is going to survive and she's talking. A lot." Miss Ames avoids looking at Kate. "They can't charge you with her murder if she isn't dead. The other news is that she confessed to lying about Joe." Miss Ames slips in a moment of eye contact, then opens a cardboard accordion file and pulls one out. "She was never pregnant. And it appears there was no sexual relationship whatsoever with Mr. Quick. She made the entire story up—we don't know why yet. They're still getting her statement. Her father's attorney is making it difficult."

Kate sits. "Difficult?" She doesn't know whether to laugh or cry. She waits for something else. Anything to salvage what's left of this hell. Staring vacantly at the hands on her knees. Her hands. Gnarled and scarred, but strong. She grunts and shakes her head. "Difficult. Difficult? Difficult would be a fucking relief." Leaning against the chair, she lets her head fall back under the florescent lights. Refusing to blink until the light burns her eyes. She feels nothing. Disconnected from her emotions like a hand severed at the wrist. She wanted to see Emma Lee happy and consider herself a good mom. Impossible now. Perhaps this was God's vindictive vengeance for killing Will. For condemning poor Joe before he even had the chance to defend himself. For passing judgment. For thinking she knew anything at all.

Miss Ames touches Kate's shoulder. "I'm going to make an appointment with the state psychologist. Temporary insanity is a good defense."

"Uncle Pat said I can stay as long as I want, and the obstetricians are probably way better in San Francisco." Em's cell cradled between her ear and shoulder as she smiles at the dented black Stetson resting comfortably on the passenger seat. Black boots on the floorboard. Huck curled up on the back seat. "Yeah, he said I can use his credit cards, whatever I need, and I still have the money Joe gave me too." Em nods as her father's Australian accent haunts her.

"Sounds like you're doing just great, angel. Told you everything would be peachy. I'll come for a visit— we can decide what to do about your mum." Uncle Pat's BMW crosses the Golden Gate Bridge.

MOANING CAVERN

November 16, 1983

Mist seeped through fog as Katherine pulled her Saab off the winding two lane. She ran to the edge of the bluff and looked out over an ocean of raw wilderness. Rolling hills like massive green swells brought to a halt and frozen in time. Rusted autumn leaves swirled as an intrusive wind held her back, suggesting she shouldn't jump. The stench of a rotting deer carcass made her nauseous, last night's indulgence of Grey Goose more likely the culprit.

She hardly felt it come up, but when it did, it spewed. Crashed over the red cliff and garnished the granite below. Bile blew back. Caught in the tangles of her over-permed hair as she shivered and gasped for her next breath. All alone on the side of the road. Not a single car had passed. How long would it be before someone came along? Stopped? Noticed she was gone?

She stepped forward, allowed her toes to cross the precipice. The next little step was the hardest. She imagined the fall. One, maybe two, hard slaps against the rock below. Savoring the momentary sting. Bleeding out. The futile last-minute will to survive, then the acceptance of that peaceful deep, dark sleep. Pain had chewed her up and swallowed. A burning in her throat forced a cough, then a sick laugh that was anything but funny. *Miserable little rich bitch. Such a cliché. A pathetic, overweight cliché.* Jumping would put an end to the constant haunting of the attack and, worse, disbelieving parents. It was the rape that resulted in an abortion nine months ago that kept the bleeding wound from healing. Kept her from leaving her dorm and not showering for up to two weeks.

Eye contact with mirrors was avoided, as was contact with her few remaining friends. Mother called it a phase, but Father put his foot down when he noticed Katherine's weight gain. The psychiatrist probably thought he was enlightening her when he explained how the trauma of sexual abuse often manifests through a preoccupation with food, and that gaining weight was a subconscious desire to become less noticeable. "*Duh.*" Katherine had glanced up at Dr. Sullivan for the first time in four sessions, then quickly averted her eyes.

"I've had it!" Father, better known as Judge Callahan, slammed his fist on the dining room table as the family shared Sunday dinner. "I'm not paying for school if you're not going to attend."

"Okay." Katherine continued to plop mashed potatoes onto her plate, then drowned them in gravy.

"I spoke to Phil at the *Chronicle*. He's got an assignment for you."

"Gee-whiz, that's great." Patrick, Katherine's older brother, looked at her—hopeful—waiting for conformation.

"I'm not qualified," Katherine said around a mouthful.

The veins on Judge Callahan's neck bulged as he set his fork down and wiped his mouth with a black cloth napkin. "If you don't take this job"—he set his hands along with the napkin on his lap—"there is a position for you at Grandpa Callahan's import business. I'm certain you're qualified to answer the telephone."

The assignment was to cover the eradication of wild cattle from the Moaning Cavern Ranch. Most of the twelve thousand acres were being subdivided, but a small section contained a massive cavern that moaned when it rained. Moaning Cavern would be open to the public by spring and making a profit by summer. The remaining herd of feral cattle, which had escaped capture year after year, had to be removed.

Editor Phil at the *San Francisco Chronicle* told Katherine that he was offering her the story due to her previous dressage experience and on the recommendation of her journalism professor at San Francisco State. Katherine knew better. There was little doubt that he owed the judge a favor.

She had never heard of Calaveras County or Moaning Cavern Ranch. Had no idea where it was located and tried not to panic or turn around when, after an hour out of San Francisco, she realized she'd forgotten the map. The gas station attendant in Jackson clicked his tongue, shook his head, and explained she'd gone the long way around. He drew her a map on a blue paper towel.

In Sheep Ranch, the road was blocked by an impenetrable flock of unsheared sheep. With one road through town—Sheep Ranch Road—barbed wire on either side prevented going around. There wasn't another human in sight as Katherine honked. Sheep didn't give a shit when she punched the horn and held it down for nearly a minute. She got out of the car. Shushed them to one side of the road. But could not get back in the car before the hostile flock surrounded her again. Their bleats more like laughter. It took twenty minutes to push through the mob, and the acrid smell rode with her the rest of the trip.

The road forked just outside of Sheep Ranch, and Katherine cursed the map. Talked to herself as she wandered the back roads. "This here's hillbilly country, and we ain't got no use for gol dern street signs or fully paved roads. Fuck dividing lines, them's for city folk. How else logging trucks gonna legally run you off the fucking road?" She was lost long before she crumpled the blue paper towel map and tossed it out.

Back and forth and back and forth, the road curved so sharply and so often it made her sick. Took almost half an hour to go eight miles. She would have turned around, went home, and explained the sincere attempt she'd made, but hadn't a clue how to get back.

Metal signs shot full of holes were strung along rusted barbed-wire fencing: *No Hunting. No Trespassing.* Katherine noticed the way the wire wrapped around trees and disappeared into their flesh but ignored the warning and pulled into a rutted drive.

She stopped at a dilapidated barn where an old man worked on a tractor that looked like it wouldn't run even if he worked on it for the rest of his life. He smelled like gasoline and wore two oily ball caps. He laughed when Katherine told him she was looking for Moaning Cavern Ranch. Said she couldn't get there from here. Called her *girlie*, then drew a map in the red dirt with his grimy finger and said, "Shoulda stayed *right* at the fork."

Sheep Ranch Road dumped her out in the quaint town of Murphy's. The sun was down, and it was too dark to find Moaning Cavern. Judge Callahan's American Express bought dinner, a room with a hot shower, and a fresh start in the morning.

***

November 17, 1983

Rain had moved east, and the sun warmed the world as Katherine drove under a log entrance that read *Moaning Cavern Ranch*. A covey of quail panicked and scattered along the gravel drive. Dust trailed her as she passed a traditional ranch-style home with a *For Sale* sign. The road descended, and at the bottom sat a corrugated metal barn. Her instructions were to meet a William Dunnigan at the barn, but that was yesterday. The Saab's obnoxious brakes squeaked like a sigh of relief when Katherine pulled up and parked.

A man with caramel-colored muscles on a five-foot frame watched from inside the barn as Katherine approached. Green high-heeled boots covered his skinny legs up to his knees. He walked toward her and removed his weathered hat, revealing tufts of hair that resembled popcorn. "You dat lady gone write a story 'bout me?" His smile was extraordinarily large.

Katherine explained that the story would focus on the process of removing the wild cattle from the ranch but didn't mention that the odds were better than good that the story would never be published. Dego Sonje just smiled and nodded. Constantly nodded, and looked down more often than not, as he spoke about anything and everything.

The rhythm of his words were hypnotic. A real Creole, "dey French be dey only kind is real Creole." Katherine petted his palomino as he rambled about guiding President Reagan and his wife on a pack trip through the Grand Canyon, years before he was "dat president." He'd been in "tree films," one with John Wayne and two he couldn't remember because he still "ain't see'd 'em." The only time he was quiet and unsmiling was when he struggled to address an envelope he had filled with cash to Reverend Jimmy Swaggart. Dego insisted the minister needed the money "so real bad," and it made him feel happy down in his bones to donate half his pay since he didn't need it anyway. Already had a good horse and a custom-built saddle.

Dego's tale of being raised in a three-story whorehouse in the French Quarter was much more entertaining than the list of Pulitzer Prize winners Katherine had been reading all summer. He claimed he didn't know his "mama or papa."

"No matta, dey all my mama, and dey all loved me. You cain't never have too much love." For the first time in nine months, Katherine smiled. She envied this

96

man who smelled like horse manure sprinkled with peppermint.

They waited almost two hours for the boss, Will Dunnigan, to arrive. Dego shared the story of meeting Will while they gathered cattle in a Louisiana swamp. Said Will was the best cowboy he'd ever seen as he filled the right side of his mouth with soft tobacco leaves until his cheek puffed to near capacity. He spit a long stream of brown juice and saddled his palomino. Katherine was about to ask him how many wild cattle he thought were on this ranch when he looked up at her and said, "Twenty-tree."

"Twenty-three what?" she asked.

"Cattle," he said, like it was the punch line to a joke and she should laugh. There was a long silence. "I been affected, I tink on my daddy's side because his mama told me in a dream. I know tings. Sometimes." He cinched his saddle. "Is just . . . comes into my head. Not always. Only sometime." It was over a full minute before Katherine realized her mouth was open.

Dego brought a short sorrel mare from her stall and tied her next to the tack room. "Dis Will's horse, but I tink is okay for you."

Katherine brushed the horse's back as Will rode up on a big gray. He didn't say a word. Just inspected the girl and rubbed his stubbled jaw with the back of his hand. He looked more like a surfer than a cowboy, with spikes of shaggy blond hair that dangled under a sweat-stained ball cap. Dego asked Will, "Is okay Miss Katrine use dis horse," in a way that sounded more like a suggestion than a question.

Will stepped off his horse without taking his eyes off Katherine.

"Katie? I'm Will. Looks like I'll be your babysitter for the next few days," he said in a raspy Australian accent. *Arrogant prick*—Katherine caught the words before they escaped. She remembered how Dr. Sullivan had explained that arrogance was a sign of low self-esteem. Then considered explaining that she'd ridden with some of the top dressage trainers in the world, that she was *not* a helpless princess. Instead, she offered her hand and a slight grin.

"I'm Katherine Callahan. Could you help me saddle this horse?" His rough hand smothered hers, and he squeezed too hard for too long. She pulled twice before he let go. He tied the gray next to the mare. A tranquilizer gun tucked in a small leather scabbard strapped to the side of Will's saddle.

"Christ, you ain't old enough to be a writer. You still in high school?"

"I attend San Francisco State."

"Now watch carefully." He looked to make sure she was watching while his words took too much time. "I'll only show ya this once." He began saddling the mare.

"What's her name?" Katherine asked.

"You never name things you might have to eat." His dark eyes reminded her of Rorschach tests.

A pack of five or six dogs ran ahead as Will rode next to Katherine and warned her about the dangers of dealing with wild cattle. His slow, menacing tone like an Australian Vincent Price.

"They're an evil lot to muster. Most renegade cattle ain't never seen a human, and they're ready for a fight

98

if they can't run. Split your horse's belly open with a horn, then when your mount goes down, they'll come back for ya. Don't ever try to outrun 'um. Get up a tree."

He looked at her as if he was waiting for an answer. Finally, she nodded.

"This ain't no holiday, lady, it's dangerous work." He described in horrific detail the way he'd lost one of his best colts when a wild old cow had stuck her horn between the colt's ribs and punctured his lung. Imitated, over and over again, the choking gasps the colt made during the half hour it took for him to die. When Katherine did not react, he unsnapped the top of his denim shirt, showed her the waxy pink scar that ran half the length of his collarbone. Said it happened when he was gathering scrub bulls in the outback.

"A bull chased me into the muck of a billabong and me horse fell. Stirred up a nest of crocks." Besides the compound fracture of his collarbone, he swore one of the buggers took a chunk of flesh out of his ass. He didn't share that scar, just trotted ahead and ordered Katherine to stay back and stay quiet.

The trail was flanked by lichen-covered granite, squatty bull pines, and oaks older than the Constitution. Dego trotted up from behind on his fancy palomino and pointed out a bald eagle for Katherine to shoot. She lifted the Pentax hanging from her neck and unfastened the lens cap. Dego kept her mare still while she zoomed in on the majestic bird.

"Beautiful." Katherine captured a dozen photos before the eagle flew off. She turned the camera on Dego. Grabbed a few headshots, then zoomed in on the chicken leg hanging from his saddle skirt. She was about to ask why but was interrupted by barking. Dego spun his horse and loped off. Katherine kicked and followed.

A narrow path wound down and disappeared into a manzanita-covered canyon. Will looked back and signaled to Katherine with his hand to wait while he followed the dogs into the canyon. Dego removed the rope from his saddle horn, then uncoiled it and built a loop. He swung it, never moving his squinted eyes away from the canyon below. Katherine straightened in her saddle and cradled the camera. Within minutes, the dogs took their barking to the next level, and Crocodile Dundee was chasing a cow and her calf through the brush. Katherine focused her camera. The excitement sent a flood of adrenaline and caused a heart-pounding high.

The instant the cow and her calf emerged from the lower trail, Will threw his rope around her horns. Wrapped the remainder of rope around his saddle horn. The slack tightened and spun the cow at Will. Dego pitched his rope under her hind legs, scooped them up, and dallyed his rope around his saddle horn. They backed their horses in opposite directions until the irate cow was taut and couldn't move. She bellowed and swung her head at the barking dogs. Thick slobber flew in all directions like a malfunctioning sprinkler. Her calf started back down the narrow trail, but a red-and-white border collie stopped him. Katherine watched in awe and missed the photo opportunity while Will tied the cow by her horns to a substantial oak. Dego released her hind legs. The cow pulled back and fought hard against the tree to no avail.

At noon, they watered the horses and ate dried apricots along a creek shaded by oaks and bordered by blackberries.

"Like apricots, Katie?" Will asked.

"I've never eaten them dried. They're good." Katherine had worked up an appetite. She popped the chewy fruit in her mouth and hoped they were an odd appetizer before the main course. When no solid sustenance was presented, she finished the pouch of apricots, then several handfuls of blackberries.

"Careful, Miss Katrin', all dat fruit gone turn you inside out."

Will laughed until he spotted fresh cattle tracks. Instantly, they were off across a field of golden grass. The dogs raced up a ridge to the south and disappeared. Will and Dego loped up the ridge while Katherine pulled on her reins and dodged squirrel holes. The camera banged against the saddle as the irritated mare jigged from being left behind. Will and Dego disappeared over the top of the ridge, and by the time Katherine arrived, there was no sign of them. Only miles and miles of rolling wilderness. She stopped and searched in every direction. Looked for tracks, but who was she kidding. She had no tracking skills. A pang of dread shot through her, then grew into a gurgle. Suddenly, her bowels began to churn and panic kicked inside her.

She rode hard to the bottom of the canyon and found a thicket of tall manzanita. A large opening offered privacy. She dismounted, ran backward, and unbuttoned her jeans just in time. The mare spooked and tried to pull away. "Whoa!" She held tight to the leather reins as the horse snorted and pricked her ears.

A low, guttural vibration came from somewhere other than Katherine's stomach. The mare reared. Jerked the reins loose. In an instant, the horse spun and was gone. Hooves hammered the hard clay—publicizing Katherine's runaway horse.

With her jeans at her knees, Katherine pulled off a boot. Fell on her ass, then removed a sock to replace much-needed toilet paper. As she turned to bury the sock at the bottom of the bushes, a twig snapped. She froze. The silence was eerie. Deep in the shadow of brush was breathing. Abnormally loud, raspy breathing. Then a low grumble and the glint of an eye. A huge, bulging eye the size of a tennis ball. It blinked, and Katherine ran for her life. For the first time ever, she ran hard and she ran far, every so often exchanging the hand that held the boot.

Gasping at the top of the ridge, Katherine stopped. Scanned the area for the monster before sitting and inspecting the cuts and scrapes on the bottom of her foot. She slipped her sockless foot back into the boot, and heat swamped her. As if it were August and not November, the air was thick. Felt like being trapped in the center of a freshly baked muffin. Sun scorched the top of her head, caused it to throb. She wished she had water. Wished she hadn't eaten the goddamn apricots. The fucking blackberries. Wished she weren't so fat.

Across a wide valley, waves of heat rolled and floated. After walking for what seemed like hours but, in reality, was only one, Katherine missed Frisco and the gloomy cold. In the distance, a rusted windmill came into view. Then a water tank sparked ambition and forced Katherine to increase her lame stride.

An amplified buzz zapped her like an electrical current when she found the mare nibbling sparse blades of grass behind the water tank. A wooden trough completed the oasis. Katherine splashed her sweaty face. Scooped water into her mouth. It worked like an elixir. She recognized her luck when she gathered the reins that the mare had dragged but not broken. A faint echo of barking pricked Katherine's ears, along with the mare's, and she climbed back into the saddle.

A short black bull was tied from his stubby horns to an oak. He didn't move a muscle when Katherine rode by. She decided to let the mare choose the way, knowing her sense of direction was better. The dogs stopped barking when Katherine approached another black bull tied to a tree. She snapped a few pictures. Was refocusing her lens when Will's filthy face filled the shot.

"You missed all the fun. Where you been?" he asked, smiling and sweating.

"Something's in the bushes over the ridge," she told him.

"A cow?" He climbed off his horse, opened his saddlebag.

"It was bigger than any cow I've ever seen. Had an eye as big as a tennis ball. And it *growled*."

"You play tennis, don't you?"

"What the hell difference does that make?"

Dego rode up, and Will's eyes puckered as he grinned. "Kate here thinks she seen a critter with an eye big as a baseball."

"Tennis ball," she said.

"You any good at it?" Will asked.

103

"At what?"

"Tennis?"

"No. I suck."

"Da steer, he 'ave only one big eye?" Dego's smile left his face. He wiped his forehead with the back of his sleeve.

"Yes."

"Cyclops."

"What the hell is it?" she asked, and Will suddenly paid attention.

"Ghost steer. Old fella work here tell me 'bout 'im. Twenty year ago when he was a calf, dey catch 'im. Castrate 'im. But next year, dey no can catch 'im. Dey chase 'im and he run off a cliff. Onto da rocks. 'Is skull, it break in half. He is dead . . . But, when dey come back, he is only gone. A ghost. No one will catch a ghost."

"Aww, bullshit." Will pulled a can of peaches from his saddlebag, popped the top, and offered it to Katherine. She shook her head no and held her stomach. "Mate, you got your visions and reality jumbled up again."

"He is real." Dego looked at Katherine, then at Will. "Believe."

"Bet half your pay?" A mischievous smile filled Will's face.

Dego watched Will drink the syrup from the can, then slurp out a peach before he agreed. "Where did you see 'im?" Dego asked Katherine.

"I can show you. He was hiding in some bushes."

The sun was sinking fast. It lit the gold leaves like hanging candles—casting a soft glow as they crossed

104

the ridge toward the brush where she hoped to prove Will wrong. Coyotes yipped close by and bristled the hairs on the back of her neck, along with two of the dogs.

"Coyotes can't hurt you if you don't pet dem," Dego said, scanning the ground for tracks.

They dropped off the ridge and into the canyon. The landscape was familiar, but every set of bushes looked the same. Katherine could not pinpoint her encounter until Will stopped his horse and looked down.

"Someone was walking, there's tracks." Will lifted Katherine's boot, then looked up at her, the light diluting his eyes. "What the hell, Katie?"

"Felt like walking. And stop calling me Katie, that's not my name."

"Felt like walking? Without your horse, and only one boot? Huh."

"You should give her a name."

"Hung up on names, ain't ya?"

"People and pets have names. You should respect that, Wilbur." She trotted away. "Think I was over here."

Before she could find the exact spot, Dego jumped from his horse and knelt. "Look." He drew a circle in the dirt the size of a salad plate. They looked down. The circle encompassed the hoofprint of one massive bovine. Will scanned the entire area as Dego pulled some feathers and another chicken leg from his saddlebag. He began to tap the items around the print.

Darkness was closing in, and the loss of light made it difficult to study the ground for more tracks. Will interrupted Dego's chanting. "Hey! We should stick Katie in the Slammer?" That familiar tinge of panic flushed through her without consent when she realized she was at the mercy of two rough men whom she knew nothing about. Will looked at her, tilted his head, and grinned. The instinct of fight or flight forced Katherine to turn her horse and ride toward the barn. She was suffocating. Her heart thumped and echoed in her ears as Will and Dego followed.

"She might like it," Will said plenty loud so Katherine was sure to hear.

"If you tink is okay." Dego sounded concerned.

She stopped her horse. Turned and faced Will, trying to hide her fear. "What's the Slammer?"

"You'll see." Will loped off.

They rode west toward the ranch headquarters. Daylight sunk into an ocean of deep violet and turned the sky into a raging fire. It was dark by the time they reached the barn, and Katherine convinced herself she was being paranoid. The Slammer was nothing to beg scared of. Dego promised.

***

November 18, 1983

For the first time in a long time, Katherine slept and dreamed without waking in a panic. An entire night without the heaviness of sleeping pills and/or a solid buzz. Doves contributed to the morning with joyous coos, but it was the lack of a hangover headache plus the aroma of coffee that brought an unfamiliar enthusiasm. Then, bacon. The smoky scent lifted her out of bed like a rising swell.

Will broke eggs into a sizzling skillet and yelled out the window, "Dego get your ass in here and eat. How'd you want your eggs, Katie?"

"I don't care." Will could not ruin the best morning since she couldn't remember when. At the table, she swatted away crumbs that looked like mouse droppings. Breathing somehow felt better—easier.

"Here ya go." Will set a plate in front of her. Three pieces of fried bacon and two eggs still in the shell. He ate standing up—like no one was watching. "How old are you?" he asked through a mouth full of runny yolks.

"Old enough to deserve some goddamn respect." She took her eggs to the hot skillet and broke them.

"Respect is something you earn, Katie."

"Whatever, Wilbur." She rolled her eyes and scrambled her eggs.

"Wilbur?" He laughed. "Me mum used to call me that. When she was *really* pissed." He shoved an entire strip of bacon into his mouth. "You pissed, Katie?"

"I want to know about the Slammer." She crossed her arms.

By six a.m., Will had the horses saddled and the Slammer loaded with two ice chests full of food, a pile of extra ropes, hay bales, three sacks of grain, and fifty pounds of dog food. Dego cranked the engine at least eight times before the Slammer finally roared to life with a belch of burnt oil. It looked more like something you'd see rumbling across an African savannah. A green military truck used in World War II to haul weapons, it had been retrofitted with several strategically placed winches to force uncooperative cattle into a large cage in the back. Katherine studied, then petted, the lifeless coyote stretched and strapped across the truck's grill. Repulsed by her admiration.

Fighting the gears and the heavy clutch, Katherine banged the Slammer up a long and rutted dirt road as Will, Dego, and the pack of dogs followed. In less than a mile, the dogs stopped, lifted their noses, and sniffed the air. An ash-colored Catahoula, named Mr. Robichaux, made his move. The pack and Dego followed.

"Wait at the top of Yayali Peak. 'Bout two more miles, there'll be a big ole cave at the top—don't go in. Yayali will eat you alive," Will said.

"Yayali?" Katherine grinned.

"Yayali is a Mi-Wuk monster that eats the children who go into his cave." Will turned and kicked his horse.

"Guess I'll be safe, then. Since I'm not a child. Asshole," Katherine said to no one.

Yayali Peak offered a spectacular view as Katherine stopped the Slammer and stepped out. Treetops blanketed the foothills as far as she could see. With a fresh roll of film, she snapped away. Walked along the road and saw the mouth of Yayali's cave. Quietly, she stepped toward it. Got as close as she could without being inside. Knelt and focused on the darkness. The click of the shutter seemed loud, then echoed. A dank coolness flowed from the cave, and with it came the scent of wet dog. Katherine could not resist the temptation and yelled, "Hello!"

"*Bonswa*!"

Kate spun. "Dego!" He rode toward the Slammer, pulling a cow at the end of his rope like an unwilling dance partner. Will arrived doing the same. Horseback and in sync, they pulled the captured cattle toward the Slammer.

"Let the ramp down, Katie!" Will yelled, and Katherine moved. She unlatched both sides, and the ramp fell hard and fast. The dogs barked and snapped at the heels of the wild cattle as Katherine photographed the entire event. Exhausted cattle waited at the bottom of the ramp while Dego placed a steel cable attached to a winch around their horns and released his rope. "Katie! The lever's behind you."

Katherine saw a knob that resembled a small gear shift. "This?" She pointed to the thing.

"Yep."

"Okay, Miss Katrine." Dego raised his hand high for Katherine to pull the lever. When she did, the motor whined and wound the cable. In no time, the unwilling animal was dragged into the Slammer. Will dismounted his horse and followed the critter in. He grabbed a coiled rope that hung from the top rail and secured the cow. They repeated the entire process until the Slammer was full.

The crew had delivered seven head of wild cattle to the corrals when Will decided the horses had had enough. Dego loaded his palomino and Mr. Robichaux into the Slammer and headed for the cabin in Tobacco Canyon. Katherine was untying the mare, who she decided to name Cyndi, after Cyndi Lauper, when she noticed the intense look that Will and one of the dogs had. They stared toward the top of a ridge about one hundred yards up. Will spun into his saddlebag and dug out a pair of binoculars. Pointed them to the top of the ridge. Katherine positioned her camera and slowly scanned

109

the same direction. A red-and-white-speckled steer with huge horns looked down at them.

"Holy shit," Will mumbled and adjusted his binoculars. "He's fucking watching us."

Katherine zoomed in until the creature filled her view. The steer's face looked like a clay sculpture that had started to melt, fell sideways, then hid under a horribly scarred hide to cover the messy mistake. His nose veered impossibly to the right. The left eye followed and bulged from the center of his skull while a hollow and withered right eye socket sat below his right ear. Massive horns were bent like twisted tree trunks—burdening him constantly. He was the Elephant Man of cattle, ostracized and alone.

"Stay here. I'll try and slip around him." Will rode away fast while Kate replaced her film and shot the monster watching her. Will emerged like a toy soldier riding up the far end of the ridge. Building his loop bigger and bigger as he closed in on Cyclops. The reality of what she was watching sunk in, and she focused the lens with shaky fingers. Her comprehension of cattle was nil, but she understood that this behemoth was something phenomenal that astonished and delighted her.

Cyclops must have sensed danger and stepped off the steep ravine before Will got within rope-throwing distance. Like a runaway semi, Cyclops crashed and plowed through the brush, leaving a swatch for Will to follow. Straight down, Will's horse sat and slid exactly like *The Man From Snowy River*, Katherine thought as she rode toward the action.

Manzanita cracked below and announced the bovine's whereabouts. The tips of his massive horns peeked over the brush, thwarting any attempt to hide. Will pushed his horse through the river of slapping and stinging branches until they disappeared under the foliage.

"He's about fifty feet to your right," Katherine yelled. The beast was as tall as Will's horse. The brush quickly turned into a tangled, impassable wall.

"*Where'd he go?*"

"I don't see him."

Cyclops had vanished into the thick growth. Will's cussing echoed through the canyon, and Katherine hoped it was due to the frustration of donating his pay to Dego and ultimately Jimmy Swaggart.

Tobacco cabin sat at the back of Tobacco Meadow. It was as basic and weathered as a one-room cabin could be. A twenty-by-twenty wood box. Just before dark, Will lit a lantern and hung it above a small kitchen table surrounded by four mismatched chairs. The white light swung, revealed, then shadowed, a woodstove, two sets of bunk beds that looked like they would not survive a heavy wind, and a small rust-stained sink topped by a shelf with a broken hand mirror.

"Dunny's out back," Will informed Katherine, then corrected himself: "You know–the crapper, shit shack. What'd you call it?"

"Bathroom," she said.

"That's dumb. There ain't no bath, and it's more like a closet than a room." He ripped a green wool blanket from the top bunk and tossed it to her. "Take it out, an' give 'er a good shake."

The smell of sour milk and mothballs engulfed her. "Outhouse, then!" She walked out.

111

"It's definitely *not* a house," Will shouted from inside. She wondered if he had been the head of the debate team back in Australia. A distant rumble interrupted her attempt at a sarcastic comeback. A beam of light cut through the dark and lit the meadow. Dogs barked. Dego gunned the Slammer and bounced the heavy truck across the rutted road to the cabin. Katherine could not wait to tell him that they'd seen Cyclops. That Will had tried to catch him, but the monster had outsmarted him. As Dego jumped out of the driver's seat and shut the door, Will walked up behind Kate. "Keep quiet about the big steer," he said, then placed his hand on her shoulder and gave it a gentle massage.

She turned around, faced him, and said, "No fucking way."

Dego smiled as he hurried toward them carrying an ice chest. Before she could confirm the reality of Cyclops, he chuckled, and said, "Ahhh, look like you seen da ghost." He set the ice chest down, slapped his knee, and broke into a from-the-gut laughing fit. "Gone be a good payday for me."

"You voodoo son of bitch." Will shook his head and lugged the ice chest into the cabin.

A thick rib eye bled into the bread and beans on Katherine's tin plate. Her appetite had returned with a vengeance as she sliced juicy chunks of meat one after the other and listened to Will give Dego a play-by-play account of the Cyclops encounter.

"I'll get that bastard if it's the last thing I do, mate." He quit eating, leaned forward, and eyed Dego. "There's a fella in Los Angeles owns carnivals and has them sideshow attractions, you know? Makes the big fella worth a pretty penny."

Dego looked at Katherine, rubbed his nose with the palm of his hand. After a long while, he shook his head. "Nope."

"Nope? What the hell's that mean?" Will asked.

"You cannot sell a ghost." Dego mopped his beans with his bread.

"Bullshit. Enough voodoo, you fuck-wit! Understand, mate? I reckon I'm the boss, and I say we ain't doin' nothin' 'til we catch the bugger." Will's face turned red.

"Okay, boss." Dego smiled and chewed.

***

November 19, 1983

Fog hid the sun while scrub oaks huddled at the bottom of Tobacco Canyon and housed a small herd of deer. They broke from their cover as Katherine, Will, and Dego approached—hooves slapping hard red clay. They'd searched and searched for Cyclops since sunrise three hours ago. More grounds-filled coffee consumed Katherine's mind as she yawned and stretched in her saddle. Dego stopped his horse. "*Laissez les bon temps rouler*!" Dego sang.

There he stood, one hundred yards above, looking down on them like a mythical creature. In an instant, the dogs spread out and up the canyon wall. Will rode at an angle to head the steer off while Dego went in the opposite direction. Katherine wasn't sure where to go or what to do. Straight ahead seemed the best photo opportunity and the safest.

The steer waited. Taunting them. Dogs came barking from every direction and the battle began. Mr. Robichaux locked down in front of Cyclops. Tried to distract and slow the steer until Will and Dego could catch up. Cyclops played along. Slowly, he lowered his head, tipped his horns, until Mr. Robichaux made a move. The dog lunged and nipped at Cyclops's nose, but the big beast was surprisingly quick. His mighty horn caught Mr. Robichaux. Flung him so hard and fast that the dog barely whimpered before disappearing into the forest. Katherine reined Cyndi behind a giant oak and readied her camera.

Cyclops ran down a steep deer trail. Deeper into the canyon with Will and Dego gaining at a breakneck speed. The remaining dogs snarled and snapped at Cyclops's nose, but never intimidated or slowed him. Katherine kicked Cyndi into a fast lope and followed.

The canyon widened. Will was gaining and the dogs backed off. He slipped his coiled rope from his saddle and in one quick motion built an extra-large loop. Dego hung back—his rope ready in his hand. The hulking creature, who'd previously enjoyed a leisurely life, was tiring fast. Riding hard alongside the steer's left hip, Will took one last swing before pitching his loop. The moment he threw, the wise brute skidded to a stop, avoiding capture by at least four feet. Cyclops turned and faced Will with that horribly disfigured snout. Faced him with that single bulging eye. Will's horse spooked, then stumbled and like a tag team, Dego rode in. The second before he threw his rope, Cyclops charged him. Katherine screamed as the steer swung his

114

massive horn under Dego's horse's belly, lifted him off all four feet, and flung him effortlessly against an oak. "Dego!"

Will's horse refused to move into the cloud of dust that hid Cyclops and the carnage. Without hesitation, Will dismounted and ran to Dego. Katherine jumped from her saddle and followed fast. As the dust settled, Cyclops was halfway back up the canyon—dogs tailing at a respectful distance. He stopped, looked back, and probably would have laughed if he could.

Dego was on his hands and knees gasping for air—pale for a dark man. Will knelt beside him. The downed horse thrashed against the oak, kicking up chunks of bark, before finding his feet.

"Dego! You okay?" Katherine squatted in front of him. He looked up with that beautiful smile, and slowly said, "You get my photo?"

She aimed her camera at his dirt-encrusted smile and took a close-up. With little effort, Cyclops could have killed Dego and his horse. Lifting her lens, Katherine searched for the bovine beast in the coagulating fog.

Holding his ribs, Dego limped to his horse. Bloody cuts and scrapes scattered the palomino's white legs. Will inspected his underbelly, but the expected gaping wound did not exist. He felt for swelling or a painful reaction, but there was none. They looked at each other, knowing the lack of damages was not due to luck.

"We'll get that crooked-faced cunt come hell or high water," Will said, mounting his horse. "Let's go if we're goin'." He left them behind. Followed the huge tracks up the canyon and into the fog. Dego led his horse a few steps before noticing the wet on his saddlebag. He unbuckled the medicine bag, looked inside, and found the shattered bottle of Rompun.

"I gone find Mr. Robichaux, den get mo' tranquilize out de barn," he told Katherine, then cringed as he pulled himself into the saddle. Sweat left tracks on his cheeks.

"Dego, are you sure you're okay?"

"Fine as frog's hair, Miss Katrine." He squeezed his ribs. "Sure hope Mr. Robichaux be fine too." Then he trotted into the forest to help his dog.

Katherine caught Will at the top of the canyon and suggested they take a break. Told him that Dego went to look for his dog and get more Rompun from the barn.

"Fuck me dead! We finally know Cyclops is headed west! Dogs are on him, and that bloody derro mucks off about his mutt?" He looked at Katherine like he expected her to agree. She did not. "We'll take a break once the old fella's in the Slammer. Okay?" He didn't wait for her consent—just rode west along the ridge.

A high noon sun burned off the fog. Will and four dogs stood in a slow creek surrounded by mossy oaks. When Katherine caught up, Will turned toward her and pressed his index finger against his lips, the universal sign to be quiet. She stopped Cyndi just before the creek. Realized Will was studying the jungle of bushes opposite the creek. A mass of poison oak bordered the creek as far as she could see. Dogs panted in the water. The entire scene looked like a Charlie Russell painting come to life. The soft rush of water spilling over stone and the chirp of cheerful birds brought contentment to the portrait.

Will pointed out the abnormally large tracks that disappeared into the thickest section of poison oak. For ten minutes, she watched Will stare at the bush. He never blinked. Finally, he said, "At's one smart son of a bitch. He'll lay up, get a good night's rest in there. Fuck wad!" He rode up the creek, and it hit Katherine that *this* was the story. The real story. Will's crusade to capture Cyclops had a Moby Dick feel. For the first time in a long time, she was itching to sit down and write the story she wanted to write. Fuck the *Chronicle* and fuck Judge Callahan.

After an hour and a half, Will had picked his way through thickets of manzanita and chamise, down a twenty-five-foot ravine, and surveyed the entire perimeter of poison oak. Strategically, he tied each of the dogs to a tree that bordered the massive patch. If Cyclops emerged, the barking dog would work as an alarm. It was his dedication, not his expertise, that Katherine began to admire when she decided to record everything and take detailed notes.

Horses were tied to trees along the creek while Will and Katherine sat on a downed log. It was the first conversation they'd had that did not include sarcasm, insults, or instructions.

Will had come to the States when he was seventeen to ride rodeo broncs and was fairly successful until a double compound fracture to his riding arm had ended his career. He hadn't graduated or attended college, but he had been taking care of himself since he'd run away at the age of thirteen. Got a job exercising racehorses on the track in Melbourne. After two years, he'd become too husky to ride the lanky thoroughbreds.

Found work mustering and breaking brumbies in the northern territory. With a six-hundred-dollar paycheck and a new bronc saddle, he'd begun his rodeo career in Australia. Beginner's luck, he called seven straight wins. He wore the last buckle he won at San Francisco's Cow Palace in 1980.

"I was there that year—showing hunter jumpers!" It felt like more than a coincident to Katherine.

"I knew you'd ridden before." Will squeezed her knee, and she jumped. "Fancy warmblood gals don't notice cowboys."

A dog barked close by and ended the chitchat. They ran—didn't bother with the horses. A black-and-tan kelpie was the culprit. He had pissed off a rattlesnake, and neither were backing down. The coiled snake was as thick as a hissing radiator hose.

"They like to shade up in the bushes." Will stepped toward the pup. "Down!" he yelled, and the animal dropped his ears, and body, and didn't bark again. "He's a beaut," Will said as he approached the snake.

"What the hell are you doing?" she asked, but Will didn't answer. He picked up a stick. Then, in an instant, he had the stick pressed against the back of the rattler's head. In one fluid motion, he snatched the snake's tail, swung it over his head, and flung the angry serpent back into the bushes. "Holy shit." She shivered as the willies crept up and down her spine.

On the way back to the horses, Will noticed new tracks. Cyclops had escaped without a sound. Will stomped and kicked and screamed like a wild stallion. Beat a boulder with his hat. Walked out and stood in the middle of the creek—boots and all. With both hands, he reached down and cupped water onto his face and

118

scrubbed it. Did his hair next. Then stepped out of the creek, slapped his hat on his head. "I need to heal. I 'spect you could use some too."

Katherine didn't respond.

"Don't talk. Just follow."

They rode up the creek about four miles in silence until Will dismounted. "Let's go if we're goin'." He finally smiled. They unsaddled and entered a forest of limestone outcroppings that sprung from the ground in angled slats. Weaved their way up and over and around and down a limestone maze. Topped a knoll. Below sat a building the size of a two-car garage. Will pulled his pocketknife as they approached and then whittled the window lock until it popped.

"What is this place?" Katherine asked.

"This is where I heal. It'll do ya good." He crawled through the window, and she followed, unconcerned that they were breaking and entering. Inside, a soon-to-be gift shop waited for tourists. Two walls of bare shelves. Empty glass cabinets. Stacks of boxes. Chrome clothes racks held a variety of Moaning Cavern T-shirts.

"This is where you come to heal? Need a shopping fix, and this is the only game in town?"

Will ignored her and unlocked a sliding glass door with his knife. "Let's go if we're goin'." He grabbed a backpack off the floor and started down the dark wooden stairs. Spurs jingled as she followed. In less than a minute, the temperature dropped and the air was comfortably cool and smelled like wet cement. After a sharp left, they were walled in on both sides by rock.

119

Will pulled two flashlights out of the pack and handed her one. "Watch your noggin."

The steps narrowed and the stone walls tightened as they sank deeper and deeper into the earth. They crossed a platform and stepped onto a spiral staircase surrounded by a heavy wire mesh that should prevent patrons from falling to their death. A single spotlight revealed small sections of inconceivable limestone formations. Ivory-colored demons. Gathered souls frozen as they screamed and reached out for salvation. Spindles and spires like polished bone. A stillness filled the ocean of emptiness. Herds of ice-colored jellyfish—their long, stringy tentacles waiting to capture prey. Down they wound for what seemed like an eternity. Fear manifested but did not stop her. She counted the steps. Fifty. Seventy-five. Two hundred. No longer part of the known world, she felt alive as their footfalls echoed the dark abyss.

"Almost there. How ya doin'?" Will had lost his sharp tone.

"I'm okay." The stairway ended at three hundred fifty-six, and Will took her hand. Lead her onto solid ground. She scanned the massive chamber with her light.

"What is this place?"

"Give me your torch and don't move," Will whispered. "Trust me."

She passed him her flashlight. He turned it off, then turned his off. Blackness swarmed them. Unable to detect even a shadow or her hand in front of her face.

"Are your eyes closed?"

She closed them. "Yes."

Something clicked. "Open them."

120

Light anointed her. The cavern was enormous. Looking up was dizzying. You could fit the Statue of Liberty in the place. Shellacked clouds of million-year-old calcium carbonate, marble, and limestone shaped the sparkling underground realm.

"This is the Moaning Cavern?" she asked.

"Yep. Next month, the place'll be filled with tourists and school kids. You're gettin' the VIP tour. Look here, Katie." Will took her hand and led her to a crystal-clear pool. Water fell from stalactites that hung like huge melting icicles. It was perfection. Without warning, he was naked and in the water. "This is healing, Katie."

"We call it skinny-dipping here." She turned and pretended to admire a massive limestone bubble the size of a VW bug. It reminded her of Chewbacca from *Star Wars*. She had her camera, but no flash, and was down to the last roll of film. Will suggested she take his picture. She ignored him and explored. Ran her hand along the smooth, cool stone wishing she could stay forever.

"You old enough to drink, Katie?"

"I don't drink," she lied.

"You gotta be over eighteen, but ya look like fifteen or sixteen." He said it as if it were a compliment. His wet feet slapped closer and closer—she prayed he was dressed.

His jeans were unbuttoned and he was shirtless. He wore the pink scar on his chest like a hallmark and leaned into her. "Your turn." So close, his breath stroked her neck.

"That's okay." No way she was getting naked in front of him.

"Don't be bashful." His hands felt big and strong and good as he squeezed her shoulders. "Use this opportunity to heal. I'll give you some privacy." With a wink, he slid down a rock and disappeared.

"Where you going?"

"Boneyard. There's a hole up top where critters fall in. Never know what ya might find." The acoustics were spectacular.

Katherine walked to the pool. Ran her hand across the turquoise water. The sound washed from side to side, then slowly faded. She pulled off her boots and rolled up her pants. The water wasn't cool but wasn't exactly warm either. It was simply soothing liquid that felt inviting. She caught a glimpse of her dirt-streaked reflection. The girl in the water shook her frizzy head at Katherine—saying, *Stop being such an uptight bitch and get your sorry ass in the water. Drown your sorrows, stupid girl.* Out of habit, Katherine looked away from herself.

"Will?"

A faint "Yeah?" came from somewhere far off.

"Just checking." She abandoned her clothes and walked in. The soft bottom felt like silk between her toes. The water sucked her in. Silently—thoughtlessly—she floated like an embryo. No yesterday. No tomorrow. Only here and now as she held her breath and sank with open eyes. Blue held her like an embrace. She didn't feel fat or ugly or angry as she bathed in the tranquility. When she surfaced, breathing felt new. Her lungs expanded. Each breath infused with an inexplicable enthusiasm. Maybe it was the water. Maybe the natural instinct of a body in fluid that triggered rebirth. Either way, Will was right, she had never felt better. Never so wide awake.

"Katherine?"

"Hang on." She swam to the shallow side and sat. Reached for her denim shirt and dried the top half of herself. Skipped the bra and buttoned her shirt. Pulling jeans on over wet skin was war. She had them to her hips when Will popped his head out of a crevice about fifty feet above.

"Was I right?"

"How'd you get up there?"

"There's tunnels and cracks all over the place. You can wiggle your way just 'bout anywhere. Look what I found." He held out a small skull.

"Oh my God."

"Yeah. Probably a Mi-Wuk kid muckin' about and fell down the hole. Didn't die right off and tried to find a way out. Tragic, aye?" He sucked back into the crevice, and she shoved her bra and panties in her boot. A woman watched her from the water. Wet curls ringed her fresh face as she grinned at herself. For the first time in nearly a year, Katherine didn't look away.

"You're beautiful, Katie. You know that?" Will set the skull on a ledge and walked over. "I mean it. I think you're lovely."

"Okay." The spiciness of his sweat touched her. When he lifted her hand, she did not resist. He looked at her hands. Stroked her fingers. An odd weakness felt good—made her warm. An inexplicable impulse bloomed, and for no good reason, she leaned toward him. His hard lips, chapped by the sun, kissed her. Kissed her neck. Shivers splashed up inside her as his sturdy hand found its way under her shirt. She

123

wondered if he could feel her heart pounding under his hand. The urge was undeniable. She had left the rape hundreds of miles away, but it was there now—with her always. Will might drown the guilt, the unwelcome sense of danger, and set her free. Panic began to conquer passion. Will guided her hand to the throbbing hardness between his legs. She jerked back like she had touched fire.

"Stop!" She felt all her breath leave her body. Without hesitation, he stopped. Pulled his shaggy hair away from his face. Tears burst and she shook her head. "I'm sorry" She was more confused than sorry.

Fury overrode fear, and she buried her head in her hands and bawled like an inconsolable child. Will rubbed her back as if he understood. When that didn't quiet her, he lifted her onto his lap and cradled her. She felt as light as a Communion wafer as he rocked her in his arms and waited patiently while she purged her demons. Fear was a stone she carried in her chest, and Will was chiseling it into something beautiful.

"You a virgin, Katie?" he whispered in her ear and kissed it.

"Yes." It felt like the truth. Rape did *not* count. No way she was going to let her first encounter with a boy ruin her chance with a man. She forced a hurried kiss to his cheek, then unbuttoned her shirt. His lips touched her nipple and warmed it with his hot breath. He rolled his tongue around and sucked on it. The urge was back in full force and kicking the shit out of anxiety as she stepped out of her jeans and into the pool.

Will shed his jeans, then stood watching her with the beginnings of an erection. "You certain, Katie?"

"I won't stop you. I promise."

His erection improved and he dove in. Wrapped himself behind her. Then reached around and worked a magical finger that set her left thigh quivering uncontrollably. She wondered if that was it—the orgasm everyone talked about—until he stepped in front of her and slid himself inside. Her heart and hips lifted without consideration and thumped against him. They floated in perfect rhythm with each stroke. Tingles swam up her legs, through her soul, and emerged in her head. They drifted into the shallows, sending waves in and out until it came from somewhere deep. The intensity grew as he moved faster, harder, on top of her. His monstrous shadow contorted against the stone wall as he consumed her.

"At a girl. There you go." He licked her earlobe. "Heal."

The rush of pure euphoria hit like an explosion from the inside out. Containing herself was not an option once every muscle in their bodies stiffened. Moans filled the cavern, and when they were through, Will said, "Now you know why it's called Moaning Cavern." Katherine's laughter echoed as she clung to Will like a barnacle.

***

November 20, 1983

Campfire smoke drifted under a canopy of oaks as the smell of sex and boiled coffee persuaded Katherine into the morning. She poked her head out from under Will's bedroll. Cyndi munched at a flake of hay, and Will was long gone. She sat up—her hair felt like a nest and she was glad to be alone.

The metal coffeepot balanced on a rock between a few remaining coals. Katherine used her shirttail like a pot holder and poured herself a cup. Grounds floated, then settled to the bottom as she sipped. Steam swirled. She inhaled. A damn good time to pick up her pen and fill some pages.

After a dozen pages, Katherine noticed the Slammer parked above camp and wondered how she had not heard Dego arrive. She walked over. Mr. Robichaux was curled on a blanket in the passenger seat. She petted and told him he would be okay. He licked her dirty hand and looked up at her as if to say, *You'll be okay too*.

It had to be close to noon when Katherine rode Cyndi by the poison oak patch. Three miles north, she found Will and Dego tracking Cyclops. The steer had headed due north, then circled back to the south as if he were intentionally attempting to mislead them. Even the dogs seemed unsure of his route—weaving back and forth—sniffing the ground and air for a solid scent.

"That fat bastard's gotta be gettin' tired," Will said, and Dego agreed. Will's frustration or obsession forced him to ride well ahead. Dego slowed his horse and rode next to Katherine. He dug into his jacket pocket, pulled out a handful of peanuts, and offered them to her.

"Thanks." She held out her hand and he filled it.

"Mr. Will possessed by dis ghost. No good. Brought yo self over here, Miss Katrin." Dego stopped his horse and waited for her to do the same. He leaned in and lowered his voice. "I gone tell you." He looked down, sighed, and shook his head. "Will . . . He gots himself a

real bad sickness. Real bad. You don't want none of it."
He handed her a second helping of peanuts, then rode
away before she could comprehend.

She was down to cracking the last nut when the dogs
went wild. They strained up an embankment to her left
and bayed like a pack of hounds on a fox. Dego stopped
his horse, pulled the bottle of tranquilizer from his
saddlebag, and handed it to Will. Dego spurred his
horse into a full gallop while Will filled two
tranquilizer darts. Slid one dart into the gun and set the
other in his saddlebag. Katherine's pulse raced as they
rode.

The dogs had gathered a wild cow and her calf. Had
them cornered against a wall of boulders. Dego swung
his rope.

"Les get 'em, boss."

Will lowered the gun. "No."

The dogs were relentless with their barking. They
never hear him. Cyclops came at Will like a freight
train with that one giant eye like a light. His horse spun
before the steer could impale his flank. They all
stumbled sideways. Cyclops stubbed his toe and went
down on his heavy chest as a grin swept across Will's
face. Katherine pointed her camera, didn't look through
it, just snapped in Cyclops's general direction. Dego
and the dogs distracted Cyclops long enough for Will to
take careful aim and fire. The dart sunk deep into
Cyclops's shoulder and caused him to spin like a
bucking bull. He snorted twice before attempting to
outrun them. They chased him out of the trees and
through a seemingly endless field as the steer gained
speed, then suddenly veered west. After about five

minutes, he was no longer just running away. He seemed to be headed somewhere in particular.

"Shot 'im again, boss," Dego yelled.

"Too much'll kill him."

Cyclops loped over a section of rolling hills and up a brushy ravine.

"Keep on him, Dego!" Will stopped his horse and reloaded the tranquilizer gun as Cyclops, Dego, and the dogs disappeared like a parade over the hill.

At the top of the hill, Katherine waited, doing her best to stay out of the way. In less than a minute, Will passed, kicking hard with each stride. He passed Dego. Passed the dogs. Gaining on Cyclops. Will hardly aimed. Held the gun at arm's length and took a long shot. The second dart hit the steer in the ass, and worry hit Dego's face.

Another five minutes passed before the tranquilizer slowed Cyclops. They kept their distance but matched his slowing stride. Farther and farther west they went until Cyclops found what he was looking for. A rusted section of wire fence that snapped with little effort when Cyclops lowered his head and forced his way through. The breaking wires, like guitar strings being tuned by an amateur, shook a long length of fence line.

At last, Cyclops had nowhere left to go. Sixty-to-seventy-foot bluffs stretched north and south for at least a mile, with only the waters of the mighty Stanislaus River below. Cyclops stopped at the edge of the bluff covered in sweat and foaming at the mouth. He raised his heavy head, then, for a brief moment, scrutinized them with that single bulging eye as he defiantly backed off the cliff.

"Will!" Katherine doubted her own eyes and looked to Will for confirmation. He only stared in disbelief. Her lungs felt like lead. Desperately, she gulped air as quick as she could. *He's fooled us again*, she hoped. The ledge had an escape route the old steer knew was below him. Dego rode dangerously close and leaned out and over the edge. He looked at them and shook his head. Katherine refused to believe it. "*No!*" She dismounted and neared the edge. The ground seemed to tilt and knocked her off-balance. She dropped to her hands and knees and crawled to the edge. Deepwater splashed and banged against the red bluffs below, drowning the possibility of a beach. Cyclops drifted downstream like an abandoned rowboat. There was no ledge. No escape route. No way out. She couldn't look away and waited for him to move. "Swim!" A sudden affinity for this animal surged through her. Guilt stung as she fought back tears and swallowed hard.

Dinner at Tobacco cabin was void of conversation. Sometimes silence is the appropriate choice. While Will washed the dishes, Katherine went outside and wrote in her journal. Frogs and crickets sang under a low-hanging moon in a black sky. Melancholy surrounded her, and after a few pages, she decided she had all the story she needed or could handle. Tomorrow the cabin would be quiet, a peaceful place to compile notes and start a rough draft of the Cyclops story.

Will came out, plucked a coiled rope off the fence post, and swung it. "Ever rope?" he asked.

"Never needed to." He sat beside her. Made her feel warm when he put his arm around her. "Are you sick?"

"Don't reckon so." He took his arm back. "Why?"

129

"Dego said you have a sickness. That I should stay away from you."

Will's face hardened—turned red. "He's a fuck-wit. You know that." He put his arm back. "I want you to come with me when I leave here next week. Got a job gathering cattle off Santa Rosa Island. You'll love it there. And it'd make a fantastic story. California State Parks stole the island from Vail & Vickers Cattle Company, and now—"

"I can't."

"Why?"

"I doubt the paper will ever publish this story. The editor only hired me because he owed my father a favor."

"Fuck them. Write the story anyhow. It'll be grand."

"I am." He had a clean citrusy smell.

"You pissed? Katherine." The way he said her name reminded her of Father O'Reilly. She cringed.

"What would I have to be pissed about?"

"Dego say anything else?" He stood and swung his rope.

"What difference does it make? He's a fuck-wit, right?" An overwhelming feeling of dread forced her toward the cabin. Will spun his rope and caught both her feet as she walked. He pulled the slack out of the rope and stopped her. From behind, he wrapped himself around her.

"You ain't leavin'. I'll tie you to a tree if I have to." He threw her over his shoulder like a sack of grain and carried her away from the cabin. Set her down next to a gnarled oak. She leaned against it as he kissed her. Resisting was an option until he put his lips behind her earlobe and stoked the fire.

"Come on, I'll teach you to rope." He took her hand, and after her roping lesson, they did things that send Catholic girls straight to hell.

***

November 21, 1983

Last night, Katherine learned she loved being cuddled while she slept. Writing helped her realize she liked herself when she was with Will and Dego. She mattered when she was with them. During breakfast, Will convinced her to spend one more day gathering and then promised Dego would drive her back to the corrals this evening. She could either spend the night in the main house or head back to the city. Her choice.

"I'll split me paycheck with ya if ya stay," Will offered.

"You bet Dego your pay. And he won fair and square," Katherine said.

"He owes me three million. We just keep bettin', makes work a bit more tolerable," Will said, and Dego nodded.

"We bet on ever't'ing, even de bird we gone see next." Dego cleared his plate. "I tink I take Miss Katrine back now. Be best for her."

The veins in Will's neck budged and his jaw tightened. He grinned. "What's waitin' at home, Katie?"

"Just . . . stuff." She sounded like a child.

The morning gather had been a success. Six head of cattle tied and ready for the Slammer. Dego had a steer roped around the horns, and Will handed Katherine his rope. She swung and swung and missed the steer's heels four times before he accidentally stepped into the open loop on the ground.

"Lift your rope!" Will hooped when she raised the tail of the rope as high as she could. "Dally, dally!" Awkwardly, she wound the end of the rope around her saddle horn and Will roared, "At's my girl!"

"I did it! Oh my God!" She laughed. A hearty, unprotected laugh. One that made her think she'd never been this happy.

"You done fine, Miss Katrin. Real fine." Dego pulled the tired steer to an oak, then rode around the tree until the rope wound the trunk twice. The steer didn't reject when Dego dismounted and tied the end of his rope—securing the animal until the Slammer arrived.

Their happiness was tangible as they ate tri-tip sandwiches back at the corrals, and they seemed genuinely impressed at Katherine's ability to swallow and then belch the alphabet. Will was a gifted yodeler, but Dego won the contest of useless skills when he stood atop the rail fence, somersaulted to the ground, then walked on his hands. Katherine was amazed; she imagined the disgusted look her mother would have given. The way her red upper lip would have curled if she were here. Father would laugh and say, "Fantastic, absolutely fantastic," and consider him no better than a well-trained pet. What would her life have been surrounded by real people like Dego and Will?

After lunch, Katherine was assigned the duty of driving the Slammer and left Cyndi behind. The diesel engine idled violently while she used the outhouse before the long, bumpy ride. From inside the outhouse, she heard Dego. His harsh tone grabbed her attention.

"You tell 'er dey truth, or I do!" Dego sounded mad.

"No worries, mate. I'll tell her. Calm down," Will answered in a high tone that felt all wrong. She listened and was zipping her pants while she rushed out to investigate. They rode away.

Only three head of fat cattle fit into the Slammer, so they left two tied. Although it had eaten on Katherine most of the day, there hadn't been an appropriate time to mention the conversation she'd overheard. Will asked her to drive the loaded Slammer back to the corrals and wait. He and Dego would go and see if Cyclops had washed up along the river. She thought it was morbid until Will explained how bacteria in the animal's gut turns to methane gas, causing them to "bloat and float." And that his skull would be worth at least a couple hundred, maybe more.

Cattle bawled continuously—fought the confines of the Slammer every now and then while Katherine waited, and waited, at the corrals. The first hour, she propped her feet out the window and napped on the Slammer's seat with Mr. Robichaux. She stretched. Walked around the corals. Considered attempting to unload the cattle herself, but untying them was too complicated and dangerous. She waited.

After two hours, worry caused her head to ache. A dead and dismembered tree lay behind the barn, and a thick patch of grass invited her to sit down and write. She brought her bag out of the Slammer and wrote.

The sun had nearly dropped by the time Will arrived leading Dego's sweaty horse. A sick feeling took hold before she could ask. He yelled in a slow, deliberate manner. "Go to the cavern. Find the phone at the gift shop. Call 911. Tell them Dego fell in the river and I cannot find him. Hurry."

Katherine ran for her car as chills blew up her spine like an icy gust of wind and scratched the back of her neck and head. She drove fast, struggling with a scenario of what could have happened. The Saab slid to a stop on the gravel in front of the gift shop. She took the stairs two at a time. Will had flipped the latches back to a locked position when they'd left. "Fuck!" she yelled. Banged and screamed for help, but knew no one was there. The stillness was eerie, and time slowed as she searched for a rock, then remembered the tire iron in her trunk.

The window broke on the second swing. She batted away the sharp edges and climbed in. Time toyed with her as moments became endless. She felt Dego's life slipping away, but not the cuts and slivers of glass in the back of her thigh. She searched behind the counter and along the wall for a phone line. Panic was taking over fast—*slow down. Focus! Fuck! Think! It had to be here. Somewhere.* And it was. Hanging just inside the hall behind the counter.

The 911 operator answered after a half dozen rings, and Katherine told her what she knew. Desperate for Dego to be okay, she prayed. On her knees, she closed her eyes and bargained with the Lord. "Please dear God, let him be okay. I promise to attend mass and go to confession from now on." She gripped her fingers. "Vengeance is mine saith the Lord, please forgive me and my evil thoughts about Allen. I swear I'll resist wrath and . . . lust." Her throat so dry it felt like swallowing broken glass. A four-wheeler skidded up outside, and Katherine ran out. It was Will.

"Did you call?"

"Yes."

"Let's keep looking." Will moved forward as Katherine climbed on behind him.

They charged along the ridge, then up a butte. Careening down steeps with little regard for safety, Will leaned into the throttle. Branches slapped and stung. Katherine stayed tucked in tight behind him until they hit the trail that ran above the twisted Stanislaus. Water roared as they searched and searched but saw no sign of Dego.

It was impossible for the ambulance to reach them. A Calaveras County Search and Rescue helicopter hovered back and forth until it was too dark. Will and Katherine held to hope well into the frigid night. She clung to him on the back of the four-wheeler until he stopped, turned off the engine and swung himself around to face her. "Dego thought Cyclops might a washed into one of the caves along the river. I didn't see him, but he could be in there. I shouldn't have let him go. He just slipped and set sail like a twig someone tossed in the current." Blackness masked his grief.

"*Tell her or I will*," played over and over in Katherine's mind as they rode the four-wheeler back to the corrals. The authentic look of concern on Dego's face when he said Will had a bad sickness. She tried to shut it off. The timing was horrible. She knew she was being immature and selfish, but the thoughts were menacing in the silence. She needed to know Will's sickness. Had the right to know.

The corrals were dark and lonely with shadows everywhere. No one from the Calaveras County Sheriff's Department had arrived yet. Cattle were still banging in the Slammer when Will killed the four-wheeler and rolled to a stop in front of the corrals.

"He told me," she said. "Dego told me about your sickness." She wrapped her arms around herself. Breath steaming with each word.

Will looked at her. Furrowed his brow.

"You should have told me." She slid off the four-wheeler and Will grabbed her arm.

"I don't have a sickness."

"I know about AIDS! I'm from San Francisco, you know!" She jerked her arm away. Gravel crunched beneath her boots, loud and obnoxious as she headed for the main house. Will stepped in front of her. He looked old.

"I ain't got AIDS or any fuckin' sickness! Swear to God." She stepped around him and walked faster. He followed. "Katherine, please stop." Tears filled his eyes. "I can't lose me best mate *and* me best girl. Christ." His voice cracked and shook something loose inside her. The world was such an unjust eternal damnation filled with senseless suffering. She stopped. Reached for him, but he had already buried himself in her chest. The shared sobs shook and warmed them.

Metal gates and latches clanged as Will and Katherine unloaded cattle from the Slammer and answered the sheriff's questions. He finished his report just after ten and left. The sky was moonless and crickets were silent.

Soon as the horses were unsaddled and fed, Will brought a bottle of blackberry wine from the tack room. They sat, shed a few more tears, and eventually drank the entire bottle.

The main house was cold as they slept on the floor of an empty living room. In a drunken stupor, Will snored behind Katherine. A *For Sale* sign stood outside the window like a billboard. Sometime in the night, Katherine woke spinning in the haze of blackberry wine. She stumbled down the tilted hall for the bathroom. Through the darkness, she heard him whisper, "Miss Katrin?" She froze. Waited for the voice in her head to return while she straddled the territory between reality and make-believe. "Miss Katrin?" The whisper was clear and had Dego's twang. She staggered toward the sound. A silhouette stood at the end of the dark hall. Her heart and head raced while she pushed against the walls—working her way toward him.

"Dego?"

His eyes glinted and he smiled as Katherine held her arms out. She hugged him—he was cold. Icy cold. "Miss Katrin, you gone get yo-self in terrible trouble you stay 'round Will. He tried killin' me today. Shoot me wit' dat dart gun when I's crawlin' 'round them slick rocks at de river. You get yo-self shed a him quick." He whispered so fast she couldn't keep up. "He done got himself lock up in Baton Rouge for messin' wit' a little girl. 'Er daddy try an' kill Will wit' his pocketknife. Dat how he get dat scar on he's chest. Ain't no crock, Miss—"

"Katie?" Will's footsteps fell fast down the hall as Dego began to float—his mouth open as if in a muted scream. A ringing in her ears grew louder and louder as time crawled around on all fours. A tingling, then suddenly Katherine felt heavy. Something tugged her from below. The moment before the world went black, Katherine knew Dego was not floating. She was falling.

***

November 22, 1983

Katherine woke naked with Will holding a cold cloth against her forehead. Mr. Robichaux snored next to the fireplace. There was a big blank spot in her memory, and the harder she tried to recall last night's events, the more her head hurt.

"Last night"—she pressed her temples—"what the hell happened?"

"You were bloody pissed."

"Pissed?" She attempted to sit up, but a severe pressure and the real possibility of her head imploding forced her to retreat. "What was I pissed about?"

"Translation—shit-faced. Found ya passed out in the hallway."

Nausea gripped her gullet, and she swallowed hard. Took several deep breaths. Closed her eyes and tried to soothe the turbulence. Set her mind back to last night. That's when the image of Dego streaked across her mind like a strange comet. "Did you see him?" she asked without opening her eyes.

"Who?" He tossed a log into the fireplace.

"Dego. He was here." Sparks fluttered up the chimney as the fire cracked.

"Naw. That was blackberry wine and wishful thinking." He brushed aside a lock of hair from her face and presented two pills and a canteen of water.

"I'm well acquainted with wine, and I've never blacked out after one bottle." She swallowed the pills and washed them down.

"You said you didn't drink." He raised his brow.

"I lied."

"Me too. The wine's kind of a blackberry concoction with a kicker. Make it meself."

"This is all just . . ." She shook her head, and the pain pulsed from side to side. "It's too much. I'm really . . . God, I feel like shit."

"Go back to sleep. I left you some coffee and biscuits on the stove." He kissed her forehead. "I'll retrieve the cattle we left tied and be back by noon."

"I need to go."

"You can write your story in peace and quiet."

"What about Dego?"

"Search and rescue are out. Nothin' more we can do."

Katherine sat up. "It's cold." She slid back under the wool blankets in the bedroll.

"Stay put. The fire 'll get goin' and I'll be back in no time." He headed for the door.

"Will?" He stopped—looked back at her. "You ever been to Baton Rogue, Louisiana?"

"Nope," he answered and left as if it weren't an odd question.

When she woke up, it was well past noon. The fire had turned to ash and she felt much better. Clothes were scattered across the floor near the front door. It took a moment to realize they were hers. Last night was still obscure. She pondered Dego. Had he seen her naked? It had to be a dream. A vivid mindfuck caused by Will's blackberry wine.

Fall was giving way to winter, but the chill felt good as Katherine walked to the barn. She found her journal inside the tack room but didn't remember leaving it there. She wondered if Will had read it. Couldn't help but go back to Dego's appearance last night. If he were alive, wouldn't he take his horse? She searched each stall. Cyndi was the only horse in the barn.

The sound of the Slammer startled her. Diesel fumes seeped into the barn as Will backed the truck up to the corrals and left it to idle while he unloaded the last two captured cattle. She gathered her courage and marched out to meet him.

"Why the hell isn't Dego's horse here? 'Cause he was here, that's why! And he—"

"Whoa, Katie." He held out his dirty palms. "I recon his horse wandered off because I didn't tie him properly. Just jumped on the four-wheeler an' took off. Settle down." He squeezed her shoulders. "They found Dego."

She considered all of it for a long while. "Where?"

"Near the dam."

It was like being punched in the heart. "I hoped somehow . . ."

"I know. Me too." He pulled her in, and they clung to each other. Will let go first. Told her he would pay whatever it cost to get Dego's body back to Louisiana and bury him properly.

"Think you could lend a hand for an hour or so? I caught a calf not a mile from here, and his mama ain't goin' far."

"Don't think I'd be much help."

"Always underestimating yourself." Will seemed serious, and for a moment, Katherine felt proud that he wanted her help.

They saddled Cyndi, and Katherine mounted. Will slid the bit into his horse's mouth as Katherine noticed movement on the hill west of the barn. She squinted hard into the sun and pointed. "Oh my God, Will, look."

He turned his head and aimed his sight with hers. "No fucking way." They stared in silent disbelief at Cyclops watching them. "You bastard." Will mounted. "Come on, Katie."

They came at Cyclops from opposite directions. The steer refused to run. Stood his ground atop the treeless hill, as the riders approached vigilantly. Will swung his rope from the front as Katherine came up from behind. The enormous beast had lost so much weight, his ribs showed through. His speckled hide looked loose against his spine and pointed hip bones. The huge head that sprang so proudly now hung low, and his giant eye seemed to be looking somewhere far away.

"What's wrong with him?" Katherine yelled.

"Just pay attention. He's waitin' 'til he can get a good shot at us!" Will threw his rope. It sailed perfectly and dropped around Cyclops's massive horns. "You're done, ya useless cunt!" Will dallied his rope around his saddle horn. Cyclops didn't move. "Rope his heels, Katherine."

Her hands shook as she unstrapped the rope from her saddle and slowly built a loop. The rope felt stiff and heavy and difficult to swing.

"Take your time and bring it around his hind legs. Now!" She threw, and the rope missed the steer's legs. "Come on, Katherine. Gather your rope and try again. You can do it." She rebuilt her loop and missed again. Twice more, she missed, until the loop fell in front of Cyclops's hind legs and Will dragged the beast forward, forcing him to step into the trap. "Lift your rope, Katherine! Lift it up." She did and had Cyclops's hind legs trapped inside her loop. "Now dally! Dally!"

Awkwardly, she wrapped the rope around her saddle horn two, then three, times, and froze. Breathing like she had just run a marathon. Cyclops never fought.

"Now hold tight. I'm gonna take him down." Will backed his horse until their ropes came tight and they had stretched old Cyclops as far as he could go. Slowly, he crashed to earth with the thud of an ancient redwood.

Will stared at the pitiful animal lying there. Not a speck of fight left in him. They waited. Every muscle in Katherine's body tense on the rope.

"He ain't even tryin'. He's givin' up." Will shook his head. "Keep your rope tight." He released his rope and shook it loose. Cautiously, he dismounted. Cyclops closed his eye as Will approached. In one swift motion, Will pulled the rope from around Cyclops's horns.

"Let him go, Katherine." He wiped the crust and flies from Cyclops's eye. Scratched between his horns and locked eyes with him for a while.

In that long moment, Katherine saw more compassion than she thought existed in the world. She laughed and cried until all doubt set sail on a teardrop. Something in the fabric of her life tore free when she released her rope and Will pulled it away from Cyclops's hind legs. She had just received the key to eternal bliss and became privy to the exact moment she fell in love.

"Bugger off now." He swatted old Cyclops on the ass. Slowly, the pitiful brute lifted his heavy horns and head, then struggled to his feet. Tears streaked her face as she stepped off Cyndi and slipped her hand into Will's. He traded her hand for an arm around her shoulder. They watched Cyclops disappear over the hill.

"You're good help. You lookin' for work, *Katherine*?" He leaned hard on the name.

She looked up at him and smiled. "I like it better when you call me Katie."

"Could use your help gathering the mob off Santa Rosa Island, Katie. But we'd need to leave tomorrow."

"Let's go if we're goin'." The words would forever haunt her.

WEST POINT

It was the goddamn eternal howling that pulled me out of oblivion. A coyote, I reckon. Several. Sometimes I drink too much. Me memory gets all jumbled—somewhat blurry between that ragged edge of sleep and awake. Warm and comfortable, like no place else. There, I could fly like goddamn Superman. Soar up into the clouds, then dive—whack the tops of pine trees, kick loose a few cones, and spook the birds. Circling the alpine meadow like a buzzard, but fully aware of my miracle flight. I'd never had a reason to want out of the fuzzy gray, but the howling wouldn't allow me to stay. It sucked me back to earth.

Me eyelids were stiff—heavier than usual—and creaked open like the lid on a coffin in a black-and-white vampire movie. Crawling out of the dirt had left me exhausted and filthy. Damp and shivering, I stood up. Me bones felt hollow, but I knew I had retained the power of flight. It came from somewhere deep inside yet far away. A conscious and focused effort that worked like a wish. I wanted to fly. Instead, I floated like a bubble, slow at first, me boots just off the frosted meadow heading west with the breeze. The goddamn coyote howled again. Louder and longer this time, sucking me toward it. Faster and faster, I went away from hunt camp and the rising sun.

It was dark by the time I arrived. And it never was a coyote. It was Em. Me precious angel was screaming to wake the dead. Me and Em's got this special bond, see. Hard to explain, really, but I promise you, we know when one of us is in trouble. I stood at the foot of her bed and saw she was bloated to beat hell and twisting like a crock in a death roll. Panic crawled up me spine. Seemed like, a minute ago, we were fishing and hunting in camp below Devil's Nose.

"Em? What's the matter? Tell Daddy!" I moved to her head and rubbed her back. She wouldn't answer, but her mum did.

"You have to push this baby out!" Kate pulled Em's knickers off.

"A baby! Bloody hell, she's only fourteen, Kate!" I couldn't believe it. The most beautiful girl I'd ever seen had turned into a scrag. Her pretty long hair was all wild and matted. She flung her head about like an ill-mannered pony and bellowed when Kate propped pillows behind her back. It felt like a dream. A nightmare.

"Push!" Kate hollered and spread two towels under Em's bum. Then she spread Em's legs. I turned away and looked out the window at nothing but dark. A sliver of moon came into view when I leaned me forehead against the pane. Weird thing was the glass wasn't cold or even cool like it should have been. It was like it wasn't there at all. I couldn't make out the barn or the

145

apple orchard I knew was filled with fall apples. Even on the darkest night, that windmill cast a shadow, but not tonight.

That old windmill. I thought we'd never get her to go. Kate and me worked on her for weeks. Cattle were out of water, and Kate wanted to sell. I didn't. Since the drought, cattle had flooded the market. They weren't worth half of what we had in them. If we sold 'em, we'd never get back what we owed the bank. Kate tried to go around me. Had a neighbor fella, Bob—what a wanker—come and snatch a load of cows to deliver to the sale yard. I fixed his wagon and hers when I come home early from brandin' at the Tejon Ranch. Rammed the front of his pickup with mine the minute I saw him at the loading chute. Me goddamn cattle in his trailer!

"Settle down, mate. Just settle down." Wanker Bob came out with his hands up like he was all innocent and I was the cops. Never call an angry Aussie *mate* if you're not mates. It just winds us up. I split his lip and busted his nose to boot. Got me cows unloaded, and that was that until Kate packed her bags. She drove as far as the front gate when Em threw a fit. Least that's what she said. Either way, we got the windmill workin' next day.

Overall, I guess Kate's a pretty good mum. Not the best wife—too bossy and always suspicious. Now she's about to be a granny if she doesn't muck it up, and she's not even forty. Em's screaming rattled me, and I looked. A little head with dark wet hair bulged between her long, skinny legs. Kate stepped between Em's knees and bent down. "Push, Em, push!"

"Did you know about this baby?" I sat at the foot of the bed and looked at me wife. "*Did you*?"

"One real hard push. Hard as you can." Kate ignored me—nothing new—and pulled me good straight razor out of her back pocket. She opened it and went to whittling near Em's bum. Jesus Christ! Poor little girl, her angel face all cherry red and about to explode. All ninety pounds of her shook when she screamed and pushed. She had the sheet all balled up in her fists, and I couldn't take it anymore. Went to the kitchen.

All the lights were on and the TV played the local news. Channel 10. The weather girl said that August was shaping up to be one of the hottest on record. "August?" It was only November. Wasn't it? Sometimes I drink too much, maybe this sheila did too. I went to turn the telly off and noticed a new sofa. It was nice enough, the tweed reminded me of Kate's hair, but this thing was too spongy. And Kate, she knew how much I loved the old sofa. Spent enough nights on it—probably had me scent—probably why she got rid of it. The remote was on the coffee table, and when I reached for it, I noticed a book with about twenty pink Post-its pokin' out. *A Midwife's Guide to Childbirth.*

I walked out on to the front porch and saw that all the firewood I'd stacked was gone. All of it! Gone. I stacked it the day before Em and me left for hunt camp. No way Kate could have burned a half a cord of wood in two days. The urge to rest overwhelmed me, and it took all me strength just to get back to Em's room.

I collapsed in a heap next to Em when Kate said, "Got him! Good girl." She set the kid, who looked like his face had been run over and flattened, on a pile of towels and tied off his umbilical cord with a zip tie.

147

"What the fuck, Kate?" was all I could muster. The little guy—all gray and chubby and slimy—opened his upturned eyes and looked right at me. He kinda looked like me when I was a baby, but all babies look alike, I guess. Funny thing was, his second and third toes were webbed—just like mine. Something wasn't right. He wasn't breathing. "You need to call an ambulance," I said. "Call an ambulance." I tried to raise me voice but couldn't. Kate went on and wiped him down with a towel, then cut his cord with me good straight razor. Like she'd done it a thousand times. Christ. Where'd she learn all this? She's delivered calves and a few foals, but come on, this was too much.

The boy finally let out a squeal like a piglet. Kinda soft and sad when Kate folded him up tight like a burrito in a beach towel I'd never seen before. We don't go to the beach. She must have bought these special for the occasion. But, when? She must have known about the baby this entire time. Where had I been? Hunt camp. Me and Em in hunt camp was the last thing I could recall. How'd I not know me angel was pregnant? Far as I know, she's not had a boyfriend. I don't know. Sometimes, I drink too much. Me thoughts get tangled. "Kate? What's going on?" I said it, but the words would not leave me mouth.

"Can I have him?" Em begged the same way she'd begged to keep a pup she lifted from a box in front of the post office.

"No." Kate set the fella on a blanket in a laundry basket, and I heard her whisper, "Sorry." Me insides curdled and I shook like a feeble old man.

Kate set the basket with the baby just outside the bedroom door, then handed Em a glass of orange juice from the nightstand.

"This will help you sleep." She began rubbing Em's tummy. "It's almost over, sweetie." She rubbed harder, and when Em closed her eyes, Kate got up and grabbed a bucket off the floor. She went back to the foot of the bed, and Em grunted but never opened her eyes. It was all I could do to raise me head and watch Kate lift a towel with a bloody blob on it out from under Em. Something that looked like a jellyfish trying to breed a piece of liver. She plopped the entire mess into the bucket, and I realized it must have been the afterbirth. When did she become such an expert at delivering babies?

I touched Em's hand while Kate cleaned her down below with a washcloth. "I love you." Me little angel was sound asleep. I reckon I fell asleep too because next thing I remember was the pinging that a cold diesel engine makes when it starts. Everything in Em's room was back to normal. No bloody towels. No bucket of afterbirth—and no baby.

I flew down the hall and out the back door in time to catch Kate loading the laundry basket in the front seat of the pickup. "Kate!" I slapped the bonnet. "Stop!" She climbed inside and about ran me over. "Stop!" Like a dog, I ran alongside the pickup until I realized she was not going to slow down or stop. I jumped into the bed just before she turned down our long gravel driveway. Down through the canyon and twelve miles to town.

149

Outside of West Point, Kate shut the headlights and turned up Cemetery Lane. Whatever she was up to—it was no good. She parked at the cemetery and got out. "*Kate? What are you doing?*" I hopped out of the bed. "Kate! This ain't right!" She stopped and looked around like she was looking for someone. She trotted to the passenger door and grabbed the handle, then lowered her head. She was crying. "Kate, please tell me what's going on." She looked up—right at me, and it was plain as day she didn't see me.

Kate opened the door and took the basket out. She's always been impulsive. Reckless, really. Like the time the babysitter said I *touched* her. Went cryin' to Kate with a load of horseshit that I had me a stiffy after wrestling with her in the barn. Said I gave her blackberry juice with alcohol in it. Kate took the girl home, then came at me with a shotgun. Told you she was reckless—shot a wad right over me head. That was ten years ago, and I'm still pluckin' pellets out me skull. Deep down, Kate knew I'd never do something like that, and when I promised to quit drinkin', she forgave me.

Halfway cross the lot, the baby started to whimper and Kate ran as best she could with the basket on her hip. She passed the cemetery gate and headed toward the chapel. The double doors were never locked, and when Kate walked in, I followed.

The chapel was lit by a single light pointed at a bloody Jesus hanging from a four-foot crucifix behind the pulpit. Kate set the basket in front of him and knelt. "Please forgive me." She stood, made the sign of the cross, and ran out. Left Jesus staring down at the innocent kid. That's when I saw him. Sitting there in the front pew was me best mate, Dego Sonje.

"Dego!" He stood up, and I hugged him. "What in the world are you doing here?" He just looked at me with his crooked grin and shook his head like he does. I was so happy to see him—until I remembered what I'd done.

"Holy shit," me voice cracked, "you're dead, mate." Dego's grin never left. "Look, sometimes, I drink too much, I never meant to hurt you." Dego went to the laundry basket and looked inside. "What's going on, mate?" I said, and he shook his head again. "Tell me. Please."

"Confess your sins or *suffer* for eternity." Dego sat right on the floor next to the baby.

"I did. I said I was sorry for what I did to you. And I am."

"Not me, Will. You hurt Em. Kate too."

"I'd *never* hurt Em. I love that girl more than anything."

"You hurt her, Will." Dego walked over and stood in front of me. "You hurt her bad."

All of a sudden, I could feel me insides rotting. I had to lay down or float away. I tried for the pew but hit the floor—closed me eyes. Fifteen years Dego and me cowboyed together. He was the best mate I'd ever had and the most honest human being I'd ever known. Guess, deep down, I knew I'd hurt Kate. Knew this time she got me good for what I'd done. Sometimes I drink too much. And that boy in the basket. "*Bloody hell*, what difference does it make? I'm dead to them anyway."

RAIL ROAD FLAT

The look on Gloria's face the first time she tried to kill
me was comical. *Comical*. Last week, Miss Alicia
asked us to use the word in a sentence. When I read my
sentence to the class, they laughed, and that was
comical too, but Gloria did not think so. She tried to kill
me again at lunchtime. She has issues, mostly with
anger and being overnourished, but I love her and I am
pretty sure she loves me. We aren't married yet. I am
only fifteen and she is sixteen, and my parents said I
have to wait until I have enough life skills to take care
of myself.

My Life Skills worksheets are always about getting jobs
so you can pay rent and buy food and be normal.
Getting a job in Rail Road Flat is not easy. There are
only four good jobs—bartender, mailman, teacher, and
principal, but they are already taken. It is hard for an
artist like me to make money in Rail Road Flat. But,
selling my drawings will be easy when Gloria and me
move to the city where people have money to buy good
art. The city has sidewalks where we can ride bikes and

sell drawings without cars flying by and dusting us out all the time. In cities, there are stores and restaurants and movie theaters you can walk to without worrying about mountain lions eating you. Our city will not have snow or power outages all the time. We will only come back to Rail Road Flat for Lumberjack Day and my birthday party in August.

My real name is August 'cause I was probably born in August. No one knows for sure. Soon as I was born, I got dumped at the First Baptist Church in West Point. That is how my mom and dad got me, and I am glad. Everyone calls me Gus, 'cept some guys call me Short Bus Gus, and that is okay—I like riding the short bus.

Gloria and me have been riding the short bus since second grade. Last year, two guys called me Short Bus, and Gloria got mad. Real mad. She tried to kill Tommy with her pocketknife. You are not allowed to bring pocketknives on the bus or to school, and she got in big trouble, and I did not get to see her for almost one month. Tommy was back in school the next day showing everyone the four stitches he got in his shoulder. I was sorry until he said he was going to kick my *beep* after school. I told him if he did, Gloria would kill him for sure. She always sticks up for me, and that is why I love her. Tommy did not beat me up. Probably, he forgot. He is not very smart.

I am smarter than my doctor thinks. Last week, I took an IQ test online and scored ninety. Ninety makes me average, and average means normal. I do not always feel normal. I asked Gloria to take the test, but she did not have time. She never has time because she always has to go home to her grandma's and wait for her mom or her dad to call from prison. They never call, and Gloria gets mad and then she has issues.

The issue I have is with people shooting our buffalo. They pay my mom and dad to come to our ranch and hunt a buffalo. It is *not* hunting. The buffalo are fenced in a meadow and cannot escape into the forest. Yesterday, while we were at church, a hunter shot my best buffalo friend, Eeyore. Murdered him! He said it was an accident, but I do not forgive him. Eeyore was an orphan and short like me. I took care of him and loved him every day, and he loved me back. Sometimes, when Eeyore was resting in the shade, I leaned on him and read out loud. Mostly, he liked comics 'cause he could eat the pages. Besides Gloria, he was my second best friend for four years until that idiot killed him. Usually, I do not cry, but now I cannot stop, and sometimes I forget to breathe. Something inside me keeps banging and banging, and it hurts. Like when you put a saddle blanket in the washer and it gets off-kilter and bangs and bangs. Mom said I will feel better—it just takes time. Dad said Eeyore was just a stupid buffalo and I should get over it.

Gloria calls me stupid when I scream. She says I overreact and that I should not scream because she is only squeezing my arm or pulling my ear and that is not killing me. When something hurts—I scream. Like today when I think about Eeyore being butchered, I want to scream. I need to talk to Gloria because she makes me happy, but she did not come to school today.

Sometimes she lets me kiss her and I feel warm and good inside, like after a big yawn. Her kisses taste like cupcakes with vanilla frosting. When we kiss, Gloria says no tongues—she does not want to have a baby. I do not want to have a baby either. I pretend I do not know about sex 'cause Gloria is nice when she thinks she is smarter than me.

After school, I rode my bike to the rez. There is only one road into the rez and a big plywood sign that says, *ROAD CLOSED, STAY OUT*, but the road is not closed. Some people in the Mi-Wuk tribe do not want outsiders driving through their land, and some cars get nails in their tires or rocks thrown at them, but not me. I only get chased by dogs. Usually, I can pedal fast and the dogs give up, but today they were chasing a deer that could not read the sign. I got to Gloria's grandma's house, but Gloria was not home.

She was not at her cousin's trailer either, the one that has a big blue tarp on the roof and cardboard where windows should be. That is where we sometimes kiss. Her cousin, Hawk, was out back throwing a knife into a tree and said Gloria was hanging with Nicole at Dustin's. I did *not* want Gloria at Dustin's house, and I did not want to cry in front of Hawk 'cause he is cool. I like the way his spiked black Mohawk flaps in the wind like a giant wing. He left the knife in the tree, then lit a cigarette and asked me why I was crying. After I explained how Eeyore got murdered and why I had to see Gloria, Hawk said he would give me a ride to Dustin's house if I gave him my bike.

Dustin's junky house is at the end of a long dirt road—mostly uphill. Too many trees. It felt dark and creepy, so I zipped my puffy coat. The house was faded like the Polaroids that my mom keeps in a shoebox. Three rusted cars and dogs on chains cluttered the yard. The dogs got mad when we pulled in. A silver pit bull with blue eyes was tied under the steps, and the whole porch shook when he jerked against his chain. Gloria and Nicole sat on a torn couch on the porch trimming weed into a plastic bowl, and Gloria jumped up.

I jumped out of the car before it even stopped and ran like in the Olympics. I hugged Gloria tighter than ever. Even though I was tired from all that running, I told her about Eeyore. She met him when her grandma brought her to my thirteenth birthday party. We fed him cake, but not ice cream. Gloria thought it might upset his stomach like it does her grandma's. She was very, very mad at the idiot for killing Eeyore. First, she made a fist, and then, the comical face . . . Her lips disappeared and her face turned red. Her black eyebrows linked like magnets. Her nostrils got wider and wider until air exploded out of them like a mad cow. She said, "How would he like it if someone shot *him*?" The silver pit bull must have seen her face, 'cause he barked at her like crazy and she yelled at him to shut up. He only barked more until she threw a snow shovel at him. When Gloria sat on the couch, I sat next to her and Nicole got up.

Nicole calls me Forest, Forest Gump, and that is how she says it. *Forest, Forest Gump.* At first, I thought she was being mean, but Gloria told me it was a compliment 'cause Forest Gump is cool. After I watched the movie, I believed her. Nicole also says I smell funky, like canned corn, and I am pretty sure that she does not like canned corn. I kissed Gloria on the cheek, and Nicole made gagging sounds, then got up and sat on the porch steps to trim.

"You're supposed to ask permission before you touch someone! That includes kissing," Gloria said.

"Can I have a kiss, please?" I leaned closer to her face and gave her my irresistible smile. I know Gloria cannot resist my smile—she told me.

"Not in front of everyone," she whispered and started clipping weed again.

"Everyone already knows I love you." That bad banging was starting inside of me.

"Shut up about it," Gloria said.

"Hawk! Is it okay if Gloria kisses me?" I yelled.

"Oh my God!" Gloria said. She was mad again.

Hawk and Dustin laughed, then shook hands, but not like my dad, like the cool guys on my baseball team. When Hawk left and Dustin went back in the house, Gloria forgot she was mad and let me kiss her cheek twice, then one time on the lips. It was like medicine. Like happy medicine.

The weed was irritating Nicole's lungs, and she wanted to go home and get her asthma medicine. When she breathed, it sounded like sawing a log when your arms are tired. Gloria told Nicole to go get their money from Dustin, then we could go. Nicole does not have her driver's license, but she had her mom's Chevy truck.

"How's Forest, Forest Gump, supposed to get home?" Nicole asked Gloria and not me.

"We can take him," Gloria said.

"I ain't drivin' the 'tard home." She looked at me and crossed her arms.

"Gus can drive." Gloria has a very good sense of humor, and that is why I love her.

"I have to go to the bathroom," I told Gloria.

"Dustin don't like anyone in the house. Go find a tree," she said. I jumped off the porch, and the dogs barked like they hated me.

The cars stunk like burning rubber and made me pull my jacket up over my nose. It was hard to find a safe place to pee—somewhere no one could see me. The forest was alive. Limbs waved every which way like giant tree people trying to tell me something important. I kept going downhill until I slipped on stupid pine needles. I hate pine needles. A low limb on a cedar tree hung like a rope, so I pulled myself up. The smell of cedar reminded me of Eeyore, and I did not want to be sad, so I sang "Jingle Bells," even though Christmas was still forty-four days away. My pee steamed and so did my breath when I said "hey" after the first chorus.

Not too far away, someone yelled, "Hey." Then a girl screamed. I zipped my zipper fast and climbed up the hill like a dog. At the house, three guys with big guns were running up the porch.

"Calaveras Sheriff's Department! Hands up!" someone yelled over barking dogs. I turned and ran away 'cause guns scare me. Spiderwebs stuck on my face, and I could not breathe. It felt like spiders were crawling all over my head, and I swatted and slapped them. At the bottom of the hill, I fell and tore my puffy coat. Feathers shot out from underneath me and scattered like a flock of spooked geese. I squeezed my eyes closed a long, long time 'cause I wanted to scream but knew I had to go save Gloria.

Gloria was in the house with Nicole and Dustin. They were all in a row. On their stomachs. On the living room floor when I walked in. Their hands were pinned behind their backs with plastic zip ties, and black storage boxes were stacked all around—almost to the ceiling. The house smelled like skunks lived there instead of people, and three white guys with haircuts like you get if you join the army or the navy looked at me.

"What the hell?" The oldest guy turned around fast and aimed a big gun at me. His shriveled face was as red as his hair, but I did not laugh. "Where did you come from?" Red looked like he wanted to kill me. I got scared and nervous and sick all at the same time, so I sat down in a lawn chair. "You best not move," Red said.

"Please do not arrest Gloria." I stood up. "She is innocent."

"No one here is innocent, including you." Red smiled, but he was not happy. He pushed me back into the lawn chair and told me to shut it or else.

Nicole wheezed and coughed, but the guy standing over her did not care; he took her cell phone out of her back pocket. He reminded me of the short bull rider I saw at the Angels Camp rodeo. He stepped over Nicole to Gloria. He frisked her like a sheriff should, but all he found was a pack of gummy bears in her sweatshirt. His Wranglers were too tight, and he could barely fit the pack in his back pocket. Police would not take your gummy bears. His cowboy boots were ripped along the sides, and when he straddled Dustin, the holes opened up like mouths. "No wallet—no firearm," he said, and held Dustin's cell phone like a trophy. "Weed ain't worth dyin' for, is it, Dustin?" Red asked.

"No, sir. Take it all."

Red slammed his gun into Dustin's back. "Need the cash too."

"What cash?" Dustin's voice was painful.

Red hit him again, but this time, he kicked him. I wished me and Gloria were at Hawk's trailer eating her gummy bears and kissing.

"Okay!" Dustin screamed. "In the dog-food bag next to the fridge!"

"I wanna see your badge!" Gloria rolled onto her back, but everyone ignored her. "None a you gots badges! You ain't *even* cops!" Gloria is smart, and that is why I love her.

A guy with big muscles and big pimples came from the back of the house with a bunch of guns. "Look what I found." He had four big guns in his arms like a load of firewood and took them outside.

"Good work, Sarge," Red said, then told Bullrider to, "Dump the dog food next to the fridge—see what's inside."

The sack of dog food must have been the big one 'cause it sounded like the load of gravel that was dumped in our driveway last week. Dustin said a very, very bad word. He said lots of bad words and banged his head on the floor until Bullrider came in with a SpongeBob lunch box. When he opened it, there was money instead of lunch. A lot of money.

"I'll load the weed and we be gone." Sarge opened the screen door just enough for his head to fit in.

Red took the lunch box, and Gloria kicked him where the sun does not shine. "My cousins are gonna kill you buttholes." Only Gloria did not say *butt*.

Red yelped like a pup when you pick them up by the neck. The lunch box hit the floor when he grabbed his nuts. Sarge ran to Gloria, and she screamed when he snatched her hair. I'd never, *ever* heard Gloria scream, and it hurt me. I screamed. When she kicked the plastic table full of dirty dishes over, it felt like they were crashing in my head. She flopped around like a fish out of water and got away from Sarge. Gloria is very strong, and that is why I love her, but Sarge stomped on her stomach and she did not fight anymore. He dragged her by her feet into the hall, and I had to do something fast.

Maybe there really was a spider on me when I was running through the forest. Maybe it bit me, 'cause all of a sudden, I got mad, then brave and strong, pretty much like Spider-Man. For sure, Gloria would love me if I beat these guys up and saved her.

I had to save her 'cause she always saves me. So, with super-spider speed, I stood up, grabbed the lunch box, and ran out the door. My legs were working excellent, and I could not stop if I wanted to. Dogs barked and rattled their chains as soon as I jumped off the porch. I slid past the crazy silver dog and made it under the stairs. The slide was perfect! Better than all the ones Coach Bryan made me do during practice last spring.

"That fat little fucker is fast." It sounded like Bullrider was on the porch above me.

161

"He has a disorder," said Red. "Just chill, I'll get him."

Under the house, the air tasted like wet dirt. I was suffocating. On the brink of death, I wriggled deeper and deeper, like a trout when they leave your hand and disappear into the darkness. My heart pounded, and I squeezed the handle on the lunch box. Time got all messed up, and I did not know if I was under the house for five minutes or five hours until sunlight coming through the slats at the back of the house stopped me. Sweat dripped down my face, but it was cold and I shivered. Stealing this money would not save Gloria. It was stupid. Don't know why I did it. What was I thinking? Maybe I am retarded. My heart shook when I saw Red's work boots and heard him say "August, come out please."

"Sorry, Red," I said over and over as I crawled out from under the house. The dogs barked so loud I did not know if Red could hear me. "I am sorry." I gave him my best irresistible smile and handed over the lunch box. With his big fist, he grabbed my puffy coat and yanked me toward him. A puff of feathers flew out of the hole, and I wanted to scream, but I did not. "I am very sorry, Red." I looked down at the red clay and dried dog turds. "I got scared when Gloria got mad. I got confused. I love her too much."

"*Goddamn it*, August." He jerked me, then let me go. Wind forced stupid pine needles to rain on us while Red opened the lunch box and inspected the stacks of hundred-dollar bills. "Get the weed in the U-Haul," he said to Bullrider and Sarge, who were waiting to pummel me.

"Why the hell are you here, August?" He kept his voice low.

"I had to talk to Gloria. It was an emergency." I kept my voice low too so no one else could hear. "An idiot murdered Eeyore."

"Your dad told me. I'm sorry. But, August, we had an agreement. Remember?"

"Yes."

"What was it?"

"I get ten percent?"

"Why do I give you ten percent?"

"So you know who to rob."

"Rob?" Red sucked his teeth, and it scared me.

"No. Not rob— Uh. Um . . ." I cannot think when I am scared."

"Dis—"

"Disinfect! I—I will not do it again, Red. I promise."

"If you *ever* show up while I'm disinfecting a grow again . . . you're fired."

I hugged him around his waist. I did not want to get fired.

"Need to zip-tie you and throw you in the house or your friends will wonder why. Don't freak out, okay?"

"Okay." I turned around and let him tie my wrists together. "Hawk told me that he is working for a grower in Valley Springs. You want to know who?" Red turned me around and looked at me for a long, long time.

"Mail the coordinates in a postcard, just like always."

The plastic ties were killing my wrists, and I wanted to scream, but I did not do it. Instead, I sucked air in my nose and blew it out of my mouth like Miss Alicia taught me. Red unzipped my puffy coat and shoved two stacks of one-hundred-dollar bills into the inside pocket. Two thousand dollars added to the six thousand four hundred buried in the buffalo boneyard makes eight thousand four hundred dollars. Soon I will have enough life skills to take care of myself. And Gloria.

Thank you for reading *Mountain Misery*. I'd love to hear what you thought of it. Please take a moment to leave a review on Amazon. A few words will determine the success or failure of an author.

Lisa Michelle is an award-winner screenwriter, author, and filmmaker. The former rodeo cowgirl and mother of two, makes her home in the Sierra Nevada. She hopes that her mostly true fiction brings meaning to the struggles of life we all share.

Discover more works by Lisa Michelle at
www.LisaMichelle2020.com

Made in the USA
Columbia, SC
06 February 2020